Preface

Although this story begins and concludes in late 2024, Mockers is primarily a novel set in North London and Hertfordshire, in post-war Britain, between 1963 and 1966. The teenage youth, born in the 40s and early 50s, were different from those people who had been involved in and experienced the Second World War.

In the early sixties those differences led to the development of a counterculture which was expressed in popular music, fashion and rebellion. A generation that was expected to shut up and enjoy the peace refused to do so. What followed was a period of incredible creativity marked by violence, risk and a sense of the old giving way to the new. It was an era that would dramatically shape the second half of the twentieth century in the UK.

This story is based on real-life landmarks and commentary that reflect real-life experiences. However, the characters are fictitious. Although some of the events took place, the story is one that could have happened. It centres around a love triangle between a young ambitious girl, Judy, who falls in love with a Rocker, Jimmy, and then after an interlude in Ireland falls in love with a Mod, Terry. It focuses on the hopes, ambitions and pitfalls of an era that treated women shamefully, especially concerning unwanted pregnancies. This was a time prior to the birth control pill becoming freely available, which liberated women around 1966.

The story begins in 2024 with a 77-year-old Judy facing death from cancer in the Watford Peace Hospice and concludes with her revealing new facts about her life to her granddaughter, Patsy, which leaves Patsy with an impossible dilemma.

Some very strong messages and issues of the time are highlighted, particularly relating to education, ambition, opportunities, society and female emancipation after the Second World War. But essentially, it's about Mods and Rockers, two wheels, speed, testosterone, aggression and youth experiencing freedom and rebellion.

The big seaside clashes between the Mods and Rockers, in Margate and Brighton took place in 1964 but for the purposes of this fictional piece of writing they are described as taking place in 1965.

The Swinging Sixties

The term Mocker was first used by the Beatles drummer Ringo Starr in the film A Hard Day's Night. When asked by a reporter if he thought his hair style was that of a Mod or a Rocker he replied, "A Mocker". It never really stuck as a label but is an entirely appropriate name for this story which is about Mods and Rockers in the sixties.

A great read, set in the early sixties dotted with factual events and music of the era. Following the journey of a group of young people, through their development into adulthood. The story takes you on a roller-coaster of events and emotions, exploring the highs and lows of the difficulties faced by young people growing up in the swinging sixties.

Jane Kimpton

What people are saying

An excellent read. The story totally captivated me as it brought back wonderful memories of my era. I found it hard to put down and return to current times. Loved it
Valerie Havard.

Mockers is a nostalgic love story that captures the youth, passion and societal pressures of young romance in the sixties. Historical detail is woven into the narrative by Will Grimsey immersing the reader into the essence of the decade using fashion and familiar music of the era.
A perfect read for fans of romance and the swinging 60's.
Kate Moore

An easy read evoking memories of the mood and music of the 60s with the fate of one of the characters following the lyrics of a song at the time.
The main character throughout told the story of how girls/women of the time emerged from the shadows of their menfolk and started to be seen and heard as individuals in their own right.
The historical facts would be a real eye-opener to the younger generation of today to realise that not everything was as easy then as it is today and also that their grandparents were once young but with a different set of problems to overcome.
Helen Burden, née Ford

Will Grimsey is 73 years old. He ha been a keen motorcyclist for over 30 years, is a fanatical Triumph enthusiast and has, in recent years, teamed up with old school mates to ride as much as possible in their retirement.

His career as a retailer spanned 45 years until his retirement in 2012 at the age of 60. Throughout his career he was known as Bill Grimsey and became the Chief Executive of leading retail chains Park n Shop Supermarkets Hong Kong, Wickes plc, Iceland, Booker and lastly, Focus Do-it-All. These appointments spanned a period of 20 years. Prior to that he was Tesco's first ever Customer Service Director and the Fresh Food Director of Budgens Supermarkets.

Upon retirement he wrote a book called *Sold Out: "Who really killed the High Street"* published in 2013.

This led to ten years during which Bill lead teams of experts to write four High Street Reviews that were presented to Government and widely recognised by Local Authorities up and down the country as templates for strategic planning. Bill travelled the length and breadth of the UK publicly speaking to assist local authorities in developing plans for the 21st Century.

He has recently decided to step back from advising on High Streets and enter a period of retirement to spend time on his passions: motorcycling, travelling, skiing and family. He has always been known as Will to his friends and family and, therefore, Bill has now been dropped in his retirement.

The inspiration for this story came when he and his biker mates saw *The Bikeriders* starring Tom Hardy at the cinema. Disappointed by the portrayal of the Hells Angels in the US as drug dealers, killers and basically thugs, Will commented to his mates that he would write a book about Mods and Rockers in the UK in the 60s, highlighting this creative period which shaped the beginning of radical cultural changes, led by a generation that wanted change following the war.

Mockers is that story.

Dedication

In memory of the Mods and Rockers that I grew up with that have now passed.

Acknowledgements

Thanks to Chris Day at Filament Publishing
for tirelessly advising, coaching
and responding to all my requests

Thanks to my current biker mates who have
contributed to this story.

Thanks to the Busy Bee Motorcycle Club,
Watford

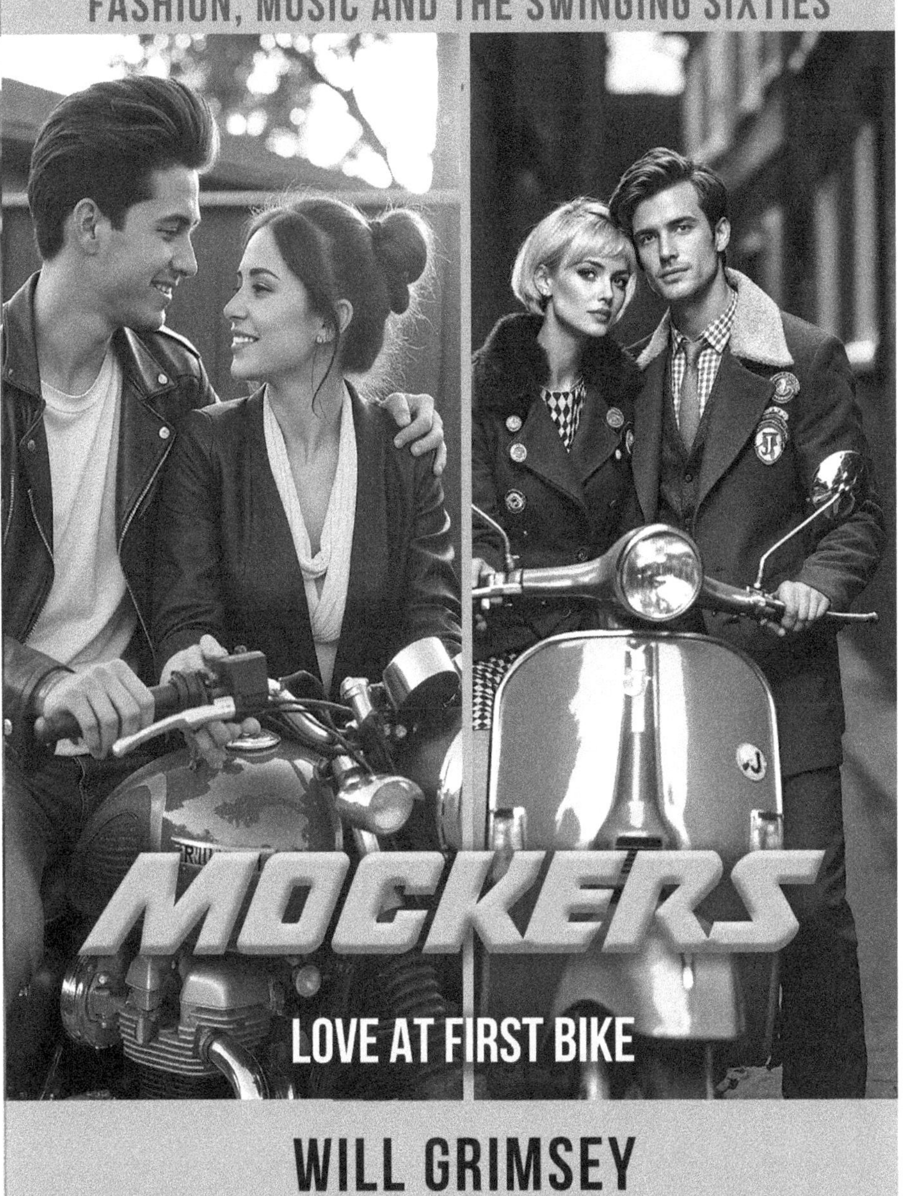
MODS AND ROCKERS
FASHION, MUSIC AND THE SWINGING SIXTIES
MOCKERS
LOVE AT FIRST BIKE
WILL GRIMSEY

Published by
Filament Publishing Ltd
14, Croydon Road, Beddington
Croydon, Surrey CR0 4PA

+44(0)20 8688 2598
www.filamentpublishing.com

ISBN 978-1-915465-78-8
Mockers by William Grimsey
© William Grimsey 2025

Printed in the UK

Contents

Musical Score

'The Wayward Wind', Frank Ifield
'Apache', The Shadows
'Bits and Pieces', Dave Clark 5
'Let There Be Drums', Sandy Nelson
'You're a Devil in Disguise', Elvis Presley
'Diamonds', Jet Harris and Tony Mehan
'Jailhouse Rock', Elvis Presley
'Can't Help Falling In Love', Elvis Presley
'I Only Want to Be With You', Dusty Springfield
'A Thousand Stars', Billy Fury
'Dynamite', Cliff Richards
'She Loves You', The Beatles
'Leader of the Pack', Shangri-Las
'Heartbeat', Buddy Holly
'Shout', Lulu and The Luvvers
'Walk on By', Dionne Warwick
'Zoot Suit', The Who
'Summertime Blues', The Who
'Can't Buy Me Love', The Beatles
'Have I the Right', The Honeycombs
'A World without Love', Peter and Gordon
'Go Now', The Moody Blues
'Can't Explain', The Who
'Anyway, Anyhow, Anywhere', The Who
'My Generation', The Who
'Yeah, Yeah', Georgie Fame and The Blue Flames
'Satisfaction', The Rolling Stones
'The Sun Ain't Gonna Shine (Anymore)', Walker Brothers
'I Got You Babe', Sonny and Cher
'Stop in the Name of Love', The Supremes

'Make it Easy on Yourself', Walker Brothers
'My Ship is Coming In', Walker Brothers
'William Tell Overture', Philharmonic Orchestra
'Long Black Limousine', Elvis Presley
'California Dreamin'', Mamas and Papas
'Help', The Beatles

Autumn 2024 *The Diagnosis*

Judy woke from a disturbed night's sleep. The small and basic room at the Watford Peace Hospice offered little luxury other than the window overlooking a grassy playing field. She sighed as the early morning light hit her face with an intensity so sharp it pierced through the thin skin of her eyelids. She turned her head a fraction and opened her eyes warily, fearful of the intense sunlight. Through sleep-bleary eyes, she could make out the silhouette of a person sitting at her bedside. The figure jumped, as though startled, and Judy felt movement on her bed cover. A hand grasped hers tightly, then the person's other hand covered both. Judy mustered all her strength and squeezed the hands. She tried to speak but had to clear her throat. She muttered, "Hello love, have you been there all night?"

Patsy, Judy's seventeen-year-old granddaughter had indeed been there all night, fretting, hardly sleeping, dozing fitfully, conscious that her grandma was at the end of her time, and desperate to prolong every moment they had left.

"Na Grandma," Patsy said. Judy knew she was lying, and Patsy knew she knew. "I got here half an hour ago; didn't want to wake you." Patsy's grandma would be concerned if she admitted the truth. Patsy had been brought up to be tough, independent and resilient, yet able to fall back on her grandma if necessary. Judy, 'Grandma', sometimes even 'Mum', had always been her rock, mentor and parent and had never thought of herself before Patsy or her other two grandchildren.

The lines around Judy's eyes reflected more pain than Patsy had ever witnessed. It hurt her like a physical ache deep in her heart to know someone she loved so dearly suffered such unimaginable pain, but she didn't want her beloved Grandma to know she was upset. The diagnosis of terminal cancer came as such a shock to them all; at the age of seventy-seven, Grandma had been so lively and outgoing, up until a few short weeks ago. Judy had to finally grit her teeth and admit that she had to tell her loved ones of the diagnosis. She resisted admitting that she'd known about the cancer for months, rather than weeks.

"Come on love, you can't fool me," Judy said with another deep sigh. "You need to look after yourself. Stop worrying about me. You have your whole life ahead of you." She paused to take another deep breath. Her sentences came out short and sharp, timed between inhalations. "Your youth will go quickly, mind my words. Don't waste any time. You have to live life to the full." A deep sigh, more of a groan, came from deep down in Judy's chest, and Patsy looked up, worried that the end had arrived suddenly and too soon for her to tell Grandma everything she needed to say to her.

Patsy bowed her head to hide the tears in her eyes. She steeled herself, conjured up a smile and looked up. "But Grandma..."

"No buts, my girl," Judy said. She tugged on Patsy's hand. "I was seventeen once. I remember the thrills and spills of life at that age, so once I've told you a few things, I want you to get out there and fulfil your dreams. Do it for me, love, in my memory, if you like."

"Tell me what things Grandma?"

A nurse knocked on the door of the little room. Judy looked around at the nurse and nodded. Patsy took the distraction as an opportunity to wipe the tears from her eyes before her grandma saw them.

"There are a few things that are important for you to know, Patsy, but that's for later. Come back this afternoon. Come and see me around 4 o'clock, there's a good girl. It's time for my meds, and then I'll want to rest," Judy muttered.

Patsy left the hospice full of sadness, mixed with intrigue. She couldn't think clearly and wondered what it was Grandma needed to tell her. She rushed off to college. She used her phone to text Brad, a boy she'd been seeing. She hoped he'd become a long-term boyfriend.

```
Hey Brad.
I need to drop by the Hospice this evening.
Grandma has something important to tell
me.
I'll be free by 8pm if that works for you.
Can't do earlier as planned.
Let me know.
Lots of love Patsy xx
```

She pressed send and ran across the road to the bus stop. Her phone pinged with a reply.

```
No worries. I'd wait all night to see U.  X
```

Patsy looked at the screen and grinned. She had no thoughts about whether people on the bus to college were staring at her and wondering why she had such a huge smile on her face.

She noticed a few curious glances in her direction, but she didn't care. Brad made her forget her worries for a moment or two; he was something special, she just knew it.

Cafe Racer
Cool is Timeless

Rockers Café Racers & The Busy Bee Café...

Monday 9th - Autumn 1963

Judy woke early on the first day of college in September 1963. She leaned over to her nightstand and picked up the alarm clock. Ten minutes before the alarm, fifteen minutes before Mum would be calling for her to get up. She was excited for her first day at Casio Hairdressing College, Watford - her first day as a proper grown-up, having left Bushey Mead Secondary Modern School earlier in the summer. When Judy got the results that she'd failed her eleven plus, the exam that determined the future of the children of her generation, it meant she didn't qualify to go to a grammar school, where she would benefit from a better quality of education and a greater chance of going on to university.

Instead, Judy and thousands of others were dumped into a system that conditioned young adults to accept work in factories or shops as their lot in life. The best hope for Judy was to forget her ambitions and set herself the task of finding a man and settling down as a mother and a housewife.

But Judy had ambition. She dreamed of running her own business one day. To begin with, a small one-man band, so to speak; a tiny salon with room in the back for tea-making facilities and a small storeroom. Maybe, once she got established, an apprentice to help sweep up and wash customers' hair no, not 'customers', she thought, 'I must get into the habit of thinking of them as clients.' Judy's dreams weren't all 'pie in the sky'. She talked everything over with Mum and Dad, and to her surprise, they said they would possibly be able to help her access that dream of a salon, as long as she passed her exams with better than just good grades. If she worked hard and excelled at her studies, the rewards would be amplified by their support.

The first step on the road to that salon, though, was to do enough to gain the skills that would enable her to access that goal. She had thought she would need all her powers of persuasion to get her parents' support through further education at college and the hairdressing course. She didn't realise it would be so easy to persuade them that she could achieve everything she set out to do. The icing on the cake was her best friend Gerry McDonald from school, who thought it was such a great idea that she also signed on to the same course.

They talked of nothing else all that summer.

"Wouldn't it be great if we both passed and got a salon together?" Gerry said, full of enthusiasm.

"Course it would! We can split the rent and set-up costs; your dad can help fit out the salon. We'll need chairs, hairdryers, sinks that allow the client to lean back to have their hair washed, shampoo, scissors..."

Judy's attention to detail may have swamped Gerry for a moment or two, but she quickly realised that Judy was the driving force in that part of their friendship, and she was the one that could make just about anything work when she put her mind to it.

Every hairdressing student needed to look good on her first day.

After a visit to the bathroom, Judy worked on her shoulder-length brunette hair, vigorously back-combing it to form a high beehive style. When she was happy with the hairdo, she sprayed a generous amount of hair lacquer over it; even the fringe over her forehead to her eyebrows didn't escape the spray treatment. Next, the makeup; black eyeliner accentuated and exaggerated the shape of her bright, emerald eyes, and dark eyeshadow and thick mascara were applied in quick, practiced strokes. Powder blush emphasised high cheekbones, and then came the final touch, ruby-red lipstick. She grabbed a tissue to place between her lips, making sure the newly applied lipstick didn't smudge, then threw the tissue into the bin under her dressing table and checked her reflection one last time. She leaned forward to examine her work. When she was happy with the result, she leaned back and winked, satisfied with her look.

Judy stepped into her petticoat and wiggled the garment over her hips. Stockings firmly attached to a suspender belt and adjusted to suit, a mauve mohair jumper, a black knee-length skirt and black kitten heel court shoes completed her outfit.

She went downstairs and grabbed a pair of flat shoes, stuffing them into her bag, just in case she was going to be standing up for a while. Judy placed the bag close to the door, ready for leaving, then she wrapped her head with a red chiffon scarf, grabbed her new black plastic coat and called out,

"Mum, I'm just going to the shop for some ciggies. I'll be back in fifteen minutes."

"Do you want your dad to take you, love?" Mum called back. "It looks like rain."

"I have my scarf on; I'll be fine for the shop," she said.

"Dad is taking me to the bus stop at Round Bush." Her dad had always driven her to the bus stop throughout her school days, as it was just a mile up the lane next door to where he worked.

"Dad, I'll need driving lessons," she had announced a few weeks before.

"You what, love?"

"I'm going to need driving lessons to get to college, and I'll need a car, too."

"Before September? You want to learn how to drive, pass your driving test and get a car, all in a matter of six weeks?" he said.

Judy was crestfallen.

"Well, when you say it like that," she said, on the verge of tears again. "It looks like I'll have to give up on college before I even start. I don't suppose you'd let me get a flat in Watford, would you?"

"Not a chance, love," came the reply.

It was worth a try, and Judy knew that having planted the seed, she would revisit the subject with him again.

She left the house for the short walk to the corner shop to buy chewing gum and cigarettes. She could hardly afford to smoke on the money from her Saturday job, but image was everything, and a cigarette enhanced a girl's aura of mystery and sophistication. Messages in the adverts claiming to help a woman keep her slim figure and declarations such as 'For people who demand only the best' made it a hard choice not to smoke. The main struggle was deciding which brand to use. Judy preferred Embassy, and she inhaled to her heart's content, just like in the advert.

The rain held off for the moment. Though it was still early, the mild September morning meant she hadn't fastened her coat, and it billowed around her as she hurried to the corner shop. The brass bell above the door rang as she went inside.

"Morning, Mr Stephens," she said, and moving across to the sweet stand, selected a packet of gum, resisting further temptation from the attractive display.

"You're not busy today?"

"Hello Judy, how are you this morning?" Mr Stephens said, looking up from his paper.

"No, we don't get busy until a little later. You're early this morning. Oh, I remember; your dad told me. You're off to college for the first time, aren't you, love?"

"That's right. I'm so excited. I can't wait to learn something practical. I want to open my own hairdressing salon one day."

She fished in her pocket for her purse. When she couldn't find it right away, she began to panic that she'd lost it on the way to the shop. Mr Stephens waited patiently as she searched her pockets again. She gave a little laugh of relief when she found the purse. "Twenty Embassy and this packet of Wrigley's gum, please," she said.

The shopkeeper turned to reach for the cigarettes from the display behind him. The peace of the morning was abruptly shattered. The thunderous roar of a motorbike as it rounded the village green and pulled up outside of the store made the shopkeeper frown. To those in the know, the noise was the unmistakable rumble of a Triumph 500 twin-cylinder motorbike engine.

To the shopkeeper, it was just another uncouth youth making a racket outside his store early in the morning. "Bloody noisy kid on a bike," he snorted.

The door opened, and the bell rang again. Judy turned with her back to the sweet stand in front of the counter full of all types of candy to see who had entered the shop. She had to raise her gaze to see the guy's face. In a fluid, practiced motion, he ducked his head as he entered the shop. When he stood up straight, Judy gasped and muttered a quiet, "Oh."

The guy's jet-black greasy hair was combed back into a quiff. He wore a scuffed black leather jacket with a mass of silver zips on the front. A white T-shirt was visible above the partly open zip, tight denim jeans were tucked into knee-high motorbike boots topped by white socks, and a white silk scarf tied around his neck helped accentuate his Adam's apple. He was clean-shaven and not dirty-scruffy like she always imagined biker-types to be. He tucked a comb into his back pocket and smiled at her.

"Morning, love," he said, his smile widening as she blushed. "You look fab. Off somewhere nice today, are we?"

Judy panicked and froze to the spot. She could feel her heartbeat in her face as the blood rushed up. She hadn't taken a breath for what seemed like minutes, and her eyes blinked a couple of times in rapid succession as she tried to curb her racing thoughts. She managed to mutter a response at last.

"First day at Casio College, actually."

She could feel the flush on her face calming down at last, and she had the distressing thought that she must look ridiculous. She tried to appear cool and sophisticated, like the Embassy advert had promised, but ended up breaking eye contact by looking down at her feet, flustered.

"That'll be two and six, love, please," the shopkeeper said, breaking into her racing thoughts.

"Oh, oh right," stuttered Judy. She fumbled in her purse, pulled out half a crown and set it down on the counter, gathered up her cigarettes and, without looking up, went to leave.

"Don't forget your gum, love," the shopkeeper called her back. He held out the packet of gum, and she turned to collect it from him.

She tried to collect herself and at least breathe normally. Then, Judy almost bumped into the tall, handsome bike rider who had moved toward the counter and suddenly accidentally blocked her path. She looked up into his dark eyes and felt her knees wobble, threatening to give way; she managed to muster the strength to smile and say,

"Excuse me. I'll be late for my bus. My dad's waiting to take me to the bus stop."

Oh, sorry, love," he said, and dodged out of her way.

"Hey, I'd be happy to give you a lift to the bus stop if you like. My name's Jimmy, Jimmy Tucker."

"That's nice of you, but my dad is expecting me home shortly to take me, so excuse me please." She blurted out her reply and rushed past the handsome stranger.

Judy was aware of a bit of a commotion as she left the shop. The shopkeeper called out, "What? Don't you want anything then?" and she felt the stranger's hand on her arm. She turned around to face the biker.

"I don't mean to startle you or be too forward, but I'd love to see you again," he said "Show me where you live, and I'll pick you up tonight around eight. We can go for a ride to the Busy Bee Café just up the road. You know, have some tea, meet some of my mates, listen to the jukebox, that sort of thing."

She shook her head 'no' and started to turn back, but he didn't let go of her arm.

He lowered his voice to a gentler tone, "I'll get you home by ten o'clock, I promise."

Judy looked into his eyes without blushing and thought for a moment. "OK," she nodded.

"But I'll meet you over there, outside the Three Horseshoes pub." She lifted her chin in the direction of the pub, just across the road on the edge of the village green.

"My dad won't like it if you come to the house." She pulled away from his hand and scurried away home, resisting the urge to look back. Her stomach seemed full of butterflies.

"You've got it love!" he called after her. "See you tonight at eight!"

Judy grinned and turned to walk backwards.

"By the way, what's your name?" Jimmy yelled.

Judy laughed and gave a little wave.

"Judy!" she called back.

Jimmy turned and went back into the shop.

"Oh, it's you again," the shopkeeper said in a gruff voice. Then he looked at the young man, and his expression softened. "Oh, you've caught something, haven't you?"

"Caught something?" replied Jimmy, a little puzzled. "Oh, you mean the girl? Yeah, I only came in to buy some fags. And look where that's taken me."

"Funny how destiny works, isn't it?" said the shopkeeper. "Me and my missus got together by chance, too. I got lost making a delivery and ended up asking her for directions. She hopped in my van to show me where I needed to go, like she'd known me forever. We've not had a day apart since."

"Yeah, destiny," Jimmy whispered, half to himself. "I take a detour through Letchmore Heath on my way to work and meet someone like her."

The shopkeeper was grinning now.

"Must be your lucky day."

Jimmy had to be called back to collect his change, and he left the shop in a bit of a daze.

"Kids," uttered the shopkeeper. "They don't know they're born."

Judy's brain was working overtime all the way home. Thoughts tumbled over themselves, and when she climbed into her dad's Morris Minor, she had nothing to say until she got out of the car at the bus stop.

"Thanks, Dad. I'll walk home this evening; there's no need to pick me up."

"OK, love, good luck today; hope it goes well."

Judy waved until the car disappeared around the first corner, then her attention turned to look for the number 311 green double-decker bus. For once, the bus arrived on time: 8:15am. With a sense of excitement for her future, Judy boarded it and made her way up the stairs.

Though she knew her friend wouldn't let her down on purpose, seeing Gerry waiting for her to sit next to her gave Judy a wave of relief. They were on their way! Gerry, Judy's best friend since they were both seven or eight, wore her peroxide-blonde hair up in a similar beehive style. Gerry had a flair for the artistic and had a black ribbon with a bow just above her fringe. Her eyeshadow was a very dark blue—almost black. Her lips were cherry red, and she wore a similar plastic coat to Judy, but in white.

"Oh, I like that bow—it looks fab against the blonde," Judy announced as she slumped into the seat next to Gerry.

"Thanks, I found the bow in Mum's sewing box, and I thought it would go with this style."

She patted the back of her hair as if to make sure everything was still where she'd placed it.

"It took ages to get it just right. I almost missed the bus. I didn't have time to go to the shops for fags; have you got any? I'll get a pack on the way to college."

Judy took out her cigarettes and offered one to Gerry. As she lit her cigarette, Gerry watched her friend.

"What have you been up to?" she said, blowing out the match.

"What do you mean?"

Gerry narrowed her eyes, smiling.

"You've met someone!" she said.

"How do you know?" Judy asked. "How do you do that?"

"I can tell. Your eyes are shining like they have real emeralds in them. You always shine when you're excited. I've known you long enough to tell the signs." Her tone sounded like she was older and wiser than the teenagers they were.

"Gerry, you'll never guess! I've had an amazing morning." Judy was bursting with excitement, an enormous grin on her face.

Gerry sat back and listened to Judy as she gushed about her romantic encounter with Jimmy, the sexy, handsome Rocker. Judy didn't even light a cigarette as she talked; she was so animated.

As the bus made its way up Watford High Street, Judy finished her tale,

"So, I'm meeting him tonight at 8pm. When we get to the Busy Bee Café, I'll ask him to get one of his mates, a good-looking one, obviously, to ride to Radlett and pick you up outside Malones newsagent at Battlers Green. He should get to you by 8.20pm. Then at least I won't be on my own. We'll be back by 10pm. He promised that already."

"OK, sounds fun," replied Gerry. "My dad will hit the roof if he finds out I've been on the back of a motorbike, but what the hell! Let's have some excitement."

The two girls made their way to Casio College in the high street. A new campus was being built north of the town but was not yet finished, so the girls and their classmates spent their first day at college in old buildings in the town centre. They expected a change from their school days and weren't disappointed—it was so different to school. Treated as young adults, they were expected to behave like responsible people.
At 5pm, after their first day in the adult world of college and further education, the girls boarded the return bus outside

Watford train station at the bottom of the high street. Their day had been filled with registration, an induction programme and health and safety, as well as getting to know other classmates, teachers, tutors and the college layout. It had been packed full of information.

A whirlwind of new stuff to learn, yet they both felt a sense of disappointment. It had been a bit of a boring day. The closest either one had come to a head of hair was when Gerry's bow came undone, and they had to sort it out in the Ladies at lunchtime.

They both looked forward to the next day when, hopefully, the course would start in earnest. Gerry made her way to the upper deck and lolled onto the front seat, with Judy right behind her. Gerry offered Judy a cigarette from her own pack, and they both lit up from the same match, grinning at each other in anticipation of the events later that evening.

Judy prepared to get off the bus at Round Bush. She turned back to her friend as she stood at the top of the stairs.

"Don't forget, 8.20pm at Malone's Newsagent. Some good-looking guy on a bike will pick you up. See you at the Busy Bee when you get there. Wear slacks for the bike ride, and don't forget a headscarf, or your hairdo will look a mess by the time you arrive," she called as she ran down the stairs.

The early-evening sun started to dip toward the hedgerows as she walked home. Greenfinches and chaffinches darted in and out of the hedges, making her smile. In places she could feel the cooler air where the sun hadn't reached under the trees, her thoughts turned toward winter, when the sun would set earlier than she'd be getting home. Judy thought about the gloomier evenings and how the walk to Letchmore Heath wouldn't be so pleasant. She would need to get a lift from Dad once the nights closed in. He had a lawnmower repair and sales business not too far from the bus stop, so when it rained or when the nights were dark early, he would drive Judy home, as he had throughout her school days.

There was something in the air as she walked home—a distinctly fresh feel to it, almost autumnal. The leaves had not yet started to turn and fall, but she could smell the difference in the air. She loved the different seasons, especially as summer turned to autumn, with the green trees getting ready to change colour, almost like they were putting on a fashion show.

But that evening, it wasn't the vibrant air that gave a bounce to her step as she fairly skipped the mile home, full of excitement as she imagined what the evening might bring.

"I'm home, Mum," she called out. "I'm starving. What's for supper? I'm going over to Gerry's tonight, if that's OK. Gerry's dad is picking me up at the Three Horseshoes, and he'll drop me off around 10."

"OK, love," her mum called from the kitchen. "Supper's nearly ready. We're just waiting for Dad to get home. You can tell us all about your first day."

"Not all of it, I can't," Judy said to herself as she went toward the kitchen.

"What's that, love?"

"Nothing, Mum, I'll set the table."

"Are you staying at Gerry's overnight, or will Dad be taking you to the bus stop again tomorrow?"

"I'm not staying at Gerry's tonight. I'll be home by 10."

"Oh yes, you just said so, didn't you?"

Judy smiled, a little concerned that her Mum did not always hear or get what she said. Shrugging, she took cutlery from the drawer to set the table for supper.

After supper, Judy did her chores, cleared the table, washed up and then went to her room to change.

Judy had been thinking of her outfit all day, and she finally decided on black slacks and the new red mohair jumper she'd not yet had a chance to wear. Her older coat, a black anorak, would be warmer than the coat she'd worn earlier, and not forgetting copious amounts of hair lacquer to hold her hair in place on the bike. Judy checked her reflection in the hall mirror. Makeup, eyeliner, lipstick and eyeshadow all passed inspection. She grabbed her bag and a headscarf.

"Bye Mum, bye Dad, I'm off to Gerry's," she called.

"Bye, love," Mum called back. "Have fun."

"Don't be late back," Dad called, raising his head above the evening paper.

"I won't be late. I'll be back around ten. I already told Mum. Bye," she called, and closed the door to prevent any further discussion.

10pm was pushing the limits on a 'school night', but, as she reminded herself, she wasn't at school anymore.

Judy walked down the street in as calm a manner as she could manage, just in case her dad was watching.

She didn't want to rouse any suspicion that she wasn't doing exactly as she said. It was five to eight. Once out of sight and certain her dad couldn't see her even if he was standing at the window, she picked up the pace and hurried to the Three Horseshoes. As she turned the corner, she slowed to a walk once more, wanting to appear aloof and confident, not too eager. Jimmy's bike stood by the village green across the road from the pub. She didn't see him at first, but her heart leaped in her chest when he shifted his position and leaned against his bike.

Once she'd spotted him, his dark silhouette appeared sharp under the streetlight, interrupted only by the embers of his cigarette. He pulled in a lungful of smoke, leaned back his head and blew the smoke into the night air to plume beneath the streetlight's glow.

Jimmy turned his head to watch Judy walking towards him. He stood up straight, flicked his cigarette into the gutter, and grinned at her.

"Hello, love, I wasn't sure you'd come. You look as lovely as you did this morning." He leaned forward to greet her.

Judy, surprised at how forward he seemed, going in for a kiss right off the bat, stiffened her demeanour and pulled away from him just a little.

'Blimey, he's going to kiss me already. That's quick!' she thought.

Jimmy caught the change in her manner and stopped short of leaning in for a kiss. Instead, he offered his hand to help her to mount his bike.

"I said I'd be here, so here I am. When you get to know me, you'll find out that when I say I'll do something, I do it."

Judy surprised herself with the sharpness of her tone.

"OK, OK, stay calm. I meant no harm by it. I'm just pleased you're here, and I've not wasted my time waiting when you're sat at home laughing at the prank you pulled on me," he said.

The small quirky turn of his lip made her heartbeat quicken as he smiled at her. She nodded acceptance of his apology and smiled back at him.

"Ever been on the back of a bike before?" Jimmy asked.

"No, I haven't, and before I do, I have something to ask you—a condition, if you like. When we get to the Busy Bee, will you get one of your mates to ride to pick up my best friend Gerry? She'll be outside Malone's newsagent, Battlers Green in Radlett in twenty minutes," Judy said in a firm tone. "If you can't, then I can't come with you. I'll have to go and meet Gerry and tell her she's wasted her time."

He shook his head to reassure her.

"No problem. That's a job for the Jokerman; he's a good rider and a lot of fun. Your friend—Gerry, was it? She'll like him."
Judy smiled, "Yeah, Gerry is her name. OK then, let's go."

Judy started to climb on the back of the bike, even before Jimmy had mounted up.

"Not so fast," Jimmy said, laughing. "I also have a few conditions about riding with me. Now listen carefully; this is important. You must never take your feet off these pegs."

He pointed to the foot pegs on either side of the bike. "You must never try to lean the bike. I know it'll feel wrong at first; you will feel an urge to lean into the corners, but you need to just keep your body in line with mine, and then you'll be OK. And the last thing is the most important. You must always hold me tight around the waist."

He placed her hands around his waist and pulled her close. Judy wasn't expecting the manoeuvre, and she gasped a little.

She quickly recovered her composure and laughed, pushing him away. She turned him around so his back faced her and placed her hands demurely on his waist.

"Surely this is how I should hold you? At all times? Won't that get a bit boring?"

"Yeah, you're going to be a handful, and no mistake," he replied with that quirky grin. "Just do as I've told you."

"Yes SIR!" Judy saluted, surprised at how comfortable she felt with the guy she'd met only a few hours before. She climbed onto the seat behind Jimmy. He waited until she was settled, then kicked started the machine. It roared into life with a deep rumble she felt through to her backbone.

She put her arms around his waist and prepared to hold on tight. At once, she had to resist an urge to hug him tighter than necessary, tighter even than he'd joked about.

Jimmy tapped the gear selector into first gear with his left foot.

He shifted from side to side to check the road for upcoming traffic, let out the clutch and set off. He took it steady around the green and up the lane towards Elstree aerodrome. He felt Judy relax behind him as they turned right up Dagger Lane. By the time they turned right onto the A41 towards the Busy Bee, he was confident in her as a passenger and decided that he could show her what Triumph, his pride and joy, could do. The A41 was a fast road, and with about two miles to the Busy Bee, Jimmy decided there was ample opportunity to open up the Triumph 500. The acceleration of the big rumbling engine combined with the way she felt as she hung onto Jimmy's body sent a series of shivers down Judy's spine.

Jimmy slowed down and pulled into the Busy Bee entrance. The bike park was already more than half full.

A variety of different motorbikes—make, model, age and condition—stood parked in lines and clusters. People milled around, chatting, looking at the bikes, catching up with friends. The steamed-up glass front of the Busy Bee café glowed from the lights inside. A flat roof overhung the walkway around the building, and a low step bordered the paving. People stood around in front of the windows, using the step as a slight advantage to see over other people's heads. Judy could hear music once Jimmy turned off his bike. She instantly recognised the track playing:

'Apache' by The Shadows. Her grin grew wider as they entered the café. The music was loud, and the buzz of conversation could be heard over the jukebox. Cigarette smoke hung heavy in the air like a smoggy morning in the middle of the city.

Quite a few people looked up when they entered the café. Only the ones playing the pinball machines ignored their arrival, concentrating on their game. Judy stayed close by Jimmy but took in all the new sights and sounds. There was a bar to get coffee, tea or soft drinks. The stools, tables and chairs were bolted to the black-and-white tiled floor, and the realisation of that amazed Judy. She'd only read about such places or seen them in films at the cinema.

A few older men—lorry drivers by the look of them—sat drinking at the coffee bar. They ignored the younger crowd and hurried out when they finished their break. Soon, the place was full of young people—bikers, mainly—but there were a few girls too. Most of the girls sported similar hairstyles to Judy's. The Shadows finished playing, and in the hush between records, Judy heard a shout.

"Watcher, Jimmy!"

Judy turned to see who had called out to Jimmy. A stocky biker with dark, swept-back hair, long sideburns and a cheeky grin came over toward them. The crowd moved out of his way as he approached.

"Watcher, Jokerman. You're just the man I wanted to see. I've got a job for you, but first, this is the lovely Judy. I met her this morning." Jimmy proudly introduced Judy.

"Hello, Judy, love; nice to meet you. Have you heard the one about…" Jokerman started to live up to his nickname, but Jimmy cut him off.

"No time for jokes yet, mate. I want you to get on your bike and go to Battlers Green, just off Willow Way in Radlett. Outside Malone's newsagent, there's a girl waiting to be picked up and brought here. Her name's Gerry. Do you know where I mean?"

"Yeah, I know it. I'm on my way. See you in twenty minutes," Jokerman replied without questioning Jimmy's request.

Jokerman hurried out of the café, hopped on his Norton and kicked it into life.

"I guess you know what you're doing." Judy looked concerned. "I hope he's a good rider; he's going for my best friend."

Jimmy looked down at Judy and pulled her gently to one side. She could see through the open door of the café. She watched as Jokerman kick-started his bike and rode it through the crowds. He seemed competent enough.

"You see that bike?" Jimmy said with a hint of pride. "That bike was produced in 1959, and it had a top speed of eighty-two miles per hour—or MPH. Rob, or Jokerman as you know him, is an expert mechanic. He takes his bikes apart for fun, and when he puts them back together again, he's found some way to improve on the performance. That bike has been bored out from 490 cc to 600 cc and can now easily do the ton."

"Do the what?" Judy asked.

"The ton, or a hundred miles an hour," replied Jimmy.

Judy clutched his arm. "He won't be doing that with Gerry on the back, will he?"

Jimmy patted her hand. "I doubt it, love. He's also an extremely safe and careful rider."

"He is?" Judy gasped, letting go of Jimmy's arm.

"Well, mostly," Jimmy said, and he laughed when Judy grabbed his arm again and glared at him.

"She'll be fine," he said. "I'll bet she loves the speed of that bike. Wait and see."

Jokerman paused at the entrance to the café bike park, looked both ways, then turned right on to the A41 off on his way to Radlett and the assignation with Gerry. As he entered Radlett, he took a right into Willow Way, then another right into Battlers Green. Sure enough, he saw a girl leaning against a wall, waiting outside Malone's. Jokerman pulled over to the kerb and killed the engine.

"You must be Gerry," Jokerman said.

"That's right, and who might you be?" replied Gerry, nonchalantly pushing herself away from the wall, trying not to appear too excited, even though she was jumping for joy inside. Judy had aced the assignment and sent a handsome biker to pick her up, just like she had promised.

"Oh, sorry, how rude of me." Jokerman exaggerated a gallant tone.

"Rob is my name—Rob Hartley, at your service. My friends call me Jokerman, as I'm always joking around." He leaned forward, took her hand in his and kissed the back of her hand. He looked up, right into her eyes, and gave her a broad grin. "But no time for that now. I'm under strict instructions to get you to the Busy Bee as quickly as possible. Have you ridden on a bike before?"

Gerry shook her head. "No, I've never had the chance."

Jokerman gave Gerry the same instructions that Jimmy had given to Judy less than an hour before. He kick-started his bike and nodded for her to get on the back.

"Hop on, love."

Gerry checked her headscarf and stepped onto the Norton's footpeg to swing her leg over the seat like an expert—or like someone that had had a few horse-riding lessons once upon a time, in her previous life back in Scotland. She wrapped her arms around Jokerman and leaned against him. He patted her hands, put the bike into first gear, looked around for traffic and headed off into the night, back to the Busy Bee.

They arrived at the café in good time. Jokerman took it steady, not going for the cheap and dangerous thrill of high speeds. He played his cards to perfection, and by the time they dismounted, Gerry felt comfortable in his presence. She was still buzzing when they reached the café door, and, on a whim, she grabbed hold of his hand. He didn't pull away, but it did make it a little awkward for him to open the café door, hold it open and allow Gerry to walk in ahead of him while still holding hands.

Gerry and Jokerman entered the Busy Bee to the sound of 'Bits and Pieces' by the Dave Clark Five. Gerry had a hard time containing herself, and when she saw Judy, she could hardly stop herself from squealing. As they said in the movies, the joint was jumping! Gerry waved at Judy across the crowded café and almost dragged Jokerman across the room, still clutching his hand.

"You're here! I'm so relieved he got you here safely," Judy said. She noticed that Gerry clung to Jokerman and nodded at their entwined hands. "I see that you two have become acquainted quickly."

Judy wasn't the only one that noticed the hand-holding. Vicky and Babs, twin sisters from Borehamwood, had also noticed. They watched the two newcomers intently, but their focus was on Gerry. With venom in their eyes, Vicky whispered something to her sister, and Babs smiled back, nodding.

"I was a bit shaky when I got off the bike, so Jokerman was just looking after me," Gerry said. She smiled and released her grip. Gerry didn't acknowledge that she'd seen the twins giving her the evil eye, but Judy knew she had clocked them when Gerry stood on tiptoe to plant a kiss on Jokerman's cheek. She gave Judy the slightest flash of a wink—a gesture they'd shared since junior school—and held the kiss long enough to make sure the two rival girls noticed.

"I don't think your girlfriends like me," she whispered to her chauffeur.

Jokerman looked around and saw the twins' expressions change from pure venom to neutral. They had been caught out unexpectedly and didn't like the fact that Gerry was already two steps ahead of them.

"Never mind those two. They're yesterday's news," whispered Jokerman as he snaked his arm around Gerry's waist and pulled her close.

She laughed and pushed him away.

"What happened to the knight in shining armour that picked me up half an hour ago?" she said, feigning a demure attitude.

"He packed up and went home. You're left with me now—a joker man in oiled leather," joked Jokerman. "I might give up jokes and collect you every night if that's a sample of payment for the ride here." Jokerman laughed and gave a glare right at Vicky and Babs, as if to say, 'what's it got to do with you two?'

Jimmy nudged Jokerman and raised his voice above the noise in the café.

"That's great, but before I introduce the two girls to the rest of the gang, let's play some pinball. I've put three records on the jukebox: Sandy Nelson, Elvis and Jet Harris and Tony Mehan. Guess which one I chose for Gerry? I think she's going to be a handful."

The four of them made their way over to the pinball machines. They didn't have to wait long for two machines next to each other to become available. The twang of guitars accompanying the lively beat of 'Let There Be Drums' added a great mood enhancer to the scene at the pinball machines. They tossed a coin for the machine they both preferred. Jokerman and Gerry had the choice. Jokerman took the coveted 'Kingpin' machine that gave the best scores. Jimmy playfully scowled as he took the second-best machine, 'Cover Girl', and they prepared to start the competition.

The boys put coins in the slots and beckoned the girls to stand at a machine. Jimmy stood behind Judy, and Jokerman pulled Gerry in front of him to 'help them to play', so they claimed.

They pushed home the coin and up popped the first ball. On cue, the girls pulled back the lever and, on the count of three, sent the ball on its way. Jimmy held Judy's hands on the flipper buttons on either side of the machine as the ball started its journey through the machine. Lights flashed, bells dinged, and the sounds of rivalry ramped up.

'You're a Devil in Disguise' by Elvis started playing, and Jimmy laughed. Gerry looked up at Jimmy.

"You put this one on because you think I'm a handful. I'll show you who's a handful!" She leaned closer to the machine and put her heart into playing the pinballs.

"Oh, you've done it now, Jimmy," laughed Jokerman. "She's all riled up! Look at her go!"

Points rolled over on tumblers on the screen of the machines. Jimmy leaned in closer to Judy every time the ball fell towards the flipper. At the optimum moment, he thrust his hip forward, pressed Judy's hand onto the button and sent the ball back up to the top of the machine.

Jokerman used the same technique with Gerry. The girls shrieked with delight each time the boys made contact, throwing their heads back, enjoying the physical closeness. They were torn between winning the contest by keeping the ball at the top of the machine and willing the ball towards the flippers so that they could relish the thrusts from behind.

The music moved on to 'Diamonds'. A crowd gathered round the pinball machines as the lights flashed and the scores clocked up. Cheers went up each time a ball was sent flying up the machine, but it was difficult to tell if the cheers were for the successful flip of the ball or the raunchy movement of the hip-thrusting movements.

Both couples were immersed in their game. The laughter and cheers increased in raucous volume, and the more the boys thrust their hips into their partners, the more excited the crowd seemed to get. The audience's loyalties divided as the game came down to the wire. The games had different bonuses but were scored similarly. It depended on luck more than skill sometimes, and Jokerman cursed when he and Gerry missed one of the better bonuses.

The crowd cheered on the couples, the excitement at fever pitch for everyone except Vicky and Babs. They sat at the tables on their own, arms crossed, wearing matching expressions of disdain.

"I don't know where those slags came from, but they'd better piss off back there," snorted Vicky. "Jokerman and I were on a break; he said he'd make his mind up last weekend. I was waiting for him to come back to me—then this cow turns up?" Vicky jerked her chin in the general direction of the newcomers.

"I know! I got the feeling Jimmy and I were making progress after I let him feel me up last week. I really thought he was going to persuade Jokerman to get back with you, too. I could just do for her." Babs was glaring at Judy.

Judy and Gerry held all the aces; they were young, fun and strangers to the world of Rockers, and that combination proved more attractive than the twins' familiar petulance. The pinball games came to an end. Jokerman got a little enthusiastic, and the game 'tilted'. Their machine shut down, the flippers stopped responding, and the last ball shot down the centre of the table to end the game. Jimmy and Judy continued playing for a few more seconds, but it made no difference: their score already topped Jokerman and Gerry's.

Jimmy put his arms around Judy's waist and picked her up, giving her a big hug. The crowd cheered. The jukebox changed records, and a familiar new sound came up. Jokerman looked around when he recognised the record. "Aw, come on! Who put this on? I mean, Wipeout? It wasn't that bad!"

"OK, now for the introductions!" Jimmy shouted over the laughter at Jokerman's expense. "Everyone, this lovely young lady is Judy. I met her just this morning, whilst on an errand of the greatest importance."

"You were buying cigarettes," responded Judy.

"Yeah, well, it was important to me," Jimmy said, laughing. "This blonde bombshell is her best mate, Gerry."

After a lot of 'Hi Judy' or 'Hello Gerry', Jimmy waved his hands for quiet. "Girls, you know me and Jokerman already, so here's a quick run-through of the rest of the gang."

Pointing towards the shortest guy in the group, Jimmy started the introductions. "This is Steve Wright, otherwise known as Turd. He's a nice guy, but Wright rhymes with shite, hence his nickname, Turd. He rides an old 1950 Indian Scout, which he restored with his own hands. The bike is a beauty, even if it is a little slow." Jimmy laughed. Turd took a ceremonious bow.

"Next is Rick Lister, nickname Bumper, on account that he rides his Ariel Leader, which looks like a car, right up on the bumper of cars in front." Bumper, a guy as tall as Jimmy with red swept-back hair and lots of freckles. Stepped forward. He also bowed. Bumper seemed a bit quieter than the rest of the crowd.

"That one is Dave Howlett, better known as Grumpy, as you can probably guess from his expression. We all think it's because his Triumph Bonneville is always leaking oil. Either that, or the fact that he can't keep up with me on my Triumph twin," Jimmy grinned. Grumpy stepped forward. He was short, stocky and clearly very strong. His grin was more of a snarl.

"Finally, Fred Haxby, known as Madman, on account of the fact that he is quite clearly mad. He's still a good rider on his Matchless 650 vertical twin, which is a mad, mad bike, so they make a 'matchless' pair, I suppose."

Madman was very tall, thin and a bit menacing, but he laughed and nodded to the girls.

"Hey, Jimmy, I tell the jokes," cried Jokerman. "Although, that matchless one, you can keep."
"OK, it's time we got you two back home. Very quickly, the girls are Sue, Lynn, Babs and Vicky. You can get acquainted next time."

Jimmy pointed in the general direction of the girls, and, as usual, he mixed Vicky and Babs up.

"Tomorrow night, the guys and I are off to the Ace Café on the North Circular. But hopefully you can join us on Wednesday for the record run night? Now, let's get you home."

"Yeah, I thought so," Babs whispered to Vicky. "Jailbait. They must be home early on a school night."

Whether Jimmy heard Babs or not, he grabbed Judy's hand and pointedly ignored the twins. Jokerman put his arm around Gerry, pulled her in for an affectionate hug and turned to smirk at Vicky and Babs. Vicky stuck out her tongue as the four left the café.

Their bikes roared into life at the first kick. They turned their headlights on, and the girls climbed on the back like expert pillion passengers. The girls held the guys firmly around the waist as they sped out of the bike park onto the A41. With a little more competition than when they arrived, the boys accelerated hard once onto the straight. They had adrenaline in their veins and a need to show off their riding skills to their girls. At the roundabout, the girls got a taste of how their new fellas could handle their machines. The lean on the tight, extended corner of the roundabout had Judy clinging desperately to Jimmy. She tried to remember what he'd told her before he took her to the Busy Bee, but her brain wouldn't work properly, and all she could do was hold on tight and trust in Jimmy. Exiting the roundabout with no traffic in sight, Jimmy and Jokerman raced neck and neck for most of the way back to Round Bush. They rode low down to limit the air resistance. Judy and Gerry could either sit up and face the fierce wind or crouch as low as possible behind their rider. Both girls trusted their guys, and they raced along on an exhilarating journey through the night.

As they approached Round Bush, Jimmy slowed down and pulled to the centre of the road to turn right to Letchmore Heath. Jokerman pulled up close on the inside, the two nodded to each other and the girls waved. Jokerman took his passenger straight on to Radlett.

Jimmy had deliberately timed the return early. They cruised down Grange Lane towards Letchmore Heath at 9:45pm. The street lighting gave scant light, and the lampposts were few and far between. Jimmy pulled up under one of the dim streetlights just outside the village. Easing the bike up onto the main stand, he dismounted and climbed back on to face Judy. He smiled. She managed a smile back but was shaking with excitement at the prospect of their first kiss. Jimmy leaned forward and took Judy into his arms. Their lips met, softly at first, and Judy could hardly catch her breath; when the kiss became more passionate, she began to feel overwhelmed and, eventually, a little scared of her own feelings rushing headlong into uncontrollable emotion. Judy pushed him away, gasping for breath. She looked him straight in the eyes.

"Go steady; this is a bit..." she said.

He nodded. "I understand. I'll not go too fast for you."

Reassured by his words, she took the front of his jacket in both hands and pulled him close again.

Her whole body tingled. Their breathing became more laboured, their eyes were closed, and they were alone in the world, completely wrapped up in themselves, in the moment.

Jimmy came up for air.

"Wow, you're amazing," he whispered.

"You're not so bad yourself," Judy whispered back.

They kissed again, their excitement escalating. Jimmy pulled back.

"Woo! Time to get you home, angel. I don't want to be in trouble for next time."

Jimmy reset himself on the bike. He pushed it off the stand, and they rode quietly down to the Three Horseshoes, where Judy dismounted.

"I'll pick you up on Wednesday at 7pm here," he said. "We can go to 'record night'. I'm sure Jokerman will make the same arrangements with Gerry."

He blew a kiss and set off, making sure there was no traffic to dodge. Judy waved at the receding back light and then turned to scurry off for home.

"Can't wait," she uttered to herself, getting in just in time for the 10pm curfew.

"Hi Mum, hi Dad, I'm back! I'm going straight to bed. I have an early start tomorrow."

"G'night love," she heard her parents call from the living room.

Judy removed her makeup and began combing her hair.

 "Oh, this is a mess," she said to the mirror. "It'll take ages to get these knots out."

Eventually, with her hair knot-free, she climbed into bed and thought about the excitement. She relived each kiss, every thrill of the bike rides, the pull of acceleration, leaning against Jimmy's back and then those kisses. What a crazy evening, full of excitement! At last, her eyelids grew heavy, and she drifted off to sleep.

The Ace Café

Tuesday 10th September 1963

Judy held out her hand and flagged down the number 311 bus. She clambered up the stairs to find Gerry. Both girls grinned at each other and shook their heads excitedly.

"What a night," Judy shrieked. "How did you get on with Jokerman when he dropped you off?"

"Bloody fantastic," Gerry replied in a voice no louder than a whisper. "We kissed and kissed some more. He was a bit of a handful." Both girls giggled at what Gerry had just said. "No, no, I meant his hands were everywhere. I had to keep willing myself to push him away, but deep down…" She didn't have to elaborate. Instead, she fluttered her eyelashes and fanned her face with her hand.

"What about you? How did it go with Jimmy?"

Judy gazed skyward.

"Just wonderful, he kissed me in a way I've never been kissed before. I could have carried on all night," she whispered, "but he was the perfect gentleman and got me home at 10pm on the dot. He arranged to pick me up on Wednesday at 7pm at the Three Horseshoes to go to record night at the Busy Bee. What about you? Did Jokerman ask you out on Wednesday?"

"Yep, same as you. I can't wait for Wednesday," replied Gerry as the bus pulled up outside Watford Station on the High Street.

The girls made their way to college, hoping to learn something about hairdressing this time.

That evening at 6.30pm, Jimmy pulled into the Busy Bee bike park after a long day at work. Jimmy was a junior draughtsman at BSP in Borehamwood during the day, and a complete bike-mad Rocker at night. He nodded to the assembled bikers, did one circuit of the bike park without stopping and headed to the exit. The others kick-started their machines and fell in behind Jimmy. They roared up the A4I, on to the A5 into London, the North Circular, and eventually to the ACE Café just short of the A40 junction.

In addition to the core crew that Jimmy had introduced to Judy and Gerry the night before, there were another ten bikers. BSAs and Royal Enfields joined the Triumphs, Nortons, Indians and a Matchless to make an impressive 16-strong pack. Jimmy rode at the front. The noise was deafening as they pulled into the bike park at the Ace Café.

Like the Busy Bee, the Ace was essentially a transport café for lorry drivers during the day. It was adopted by bikers by night and at weekends. It was bigger than the Busy Bee, with a jukebox, pinball machines, an array of bike memorabilia and pictures covering the walls. The management took advantage of the diversity of their client base and decorated to suit, celebrating the Rockers and bikers, encouraging them to keep coming back. The bikers that frequented these cafés in the sixties were known as 'Café Racers', often racing each other between cafés. The tables, chairs and bar stools were bolted to the black-and-white tiled floor, just like at the Busy Bee. The Ace was packed that night—Tuesday being bikers' night—with no girls in sight. There must have been close to 100 bikes in the bike park as Jimmy and his crew rolled in.

Every Tuesday, bikers from all over greater London turned up at the Ace to chat about bikes, look at each other's bikes—sometimes with envy—listen to good music and generally catch up with friends.

Occasionally, someone would suggest a spontaneous race. The bikers who were up for it, either to showcase the speed of their bike or their skills at riding, took off from the bike park and headed off towards Neasden on the North Circular and back at breathtaking speeds. There were no prizes to be won, just the satisfaction of making it back without damage or injury and the attention from the spectators when they arrived back at the front of the pack. Unfortunately, many bikers met their death on these escapades as they pushed their machines to the limit. That evening there were around twenty bikers from Ryka's Café at Box Hill in Surrey already at the café.

As Jimmy and the crew from the Busy Bee parked up, they were greeted by a bunch of regulars from the Ace led by Phil, nicknamed Speedy.

"Hey, Jimmy!" yelled Speedy as he approached, "We've got a bunch of lads in from Ryka's at Box Hill; should be a good night."

"Sounds good," replied Jimmy as he greeted Speedy with a slap on the back. They headed for the café. Inside, the air was thick with cigarette smoke and a faint whiff of oil that seemed to ooze from the bikers' leather jackets. They could hear the jukebox before they got to the door. Elvis Presley was singing 'Jailhouse Rock'. Speedy and Jimmy approached the door and stood back, waiting for blokes who were coming out. They turned back around as the sounds of a scuffle broke out inside the café.

One of the Ryka's boys had spotted Turd's old Indian Scout bike in the bike park. He pointed out the bike and started laughing with his mates.

"What're you laughing at, mate?" Turd growled a challenge. He eyeballed the guy, his lip twisted in a sneer, fists at his sides, daring him to make a move.

The guy that had started the laughing replied, "Nothing, mate. We were wondering whose bike it is. Now we know, we think that bike would be too much for a titch like you to handle."

Madman put a hand on Turd's arm to guide him away from the trouble.

"Leave it, Turd. He's not worth it."

When he heard Turd's nickname, the troublemaker roared with laughter. With an audience already engaged and drawing in more guys who heard the start of the commotion, he shouted for the benefit of his mates. "Not only does he ride an old crock of shit for a bike, but his name's Turd, too. I can't tell which one stinks the most; the bike or the Turd!"

"Fuck you!" yelled Turd as his forehead smashed on the guy's nose, instantly breaking it, sending a spray of blood and snot across the guy's face, putting a stop to the laughter. An all-out fight erupted inside the Ace.

Madman sighed, "Here we go again," as he flattened two oncoming guys with a fist to one's nose and an elbow to the chin of the other.

The two guys Jimmy and Speedy had waited for at the door to the café shoved past Jimmy, knocking him into Speedy.

"Hey! Watch what you're doing!" shouted Jimmy, and his eyes widened as he realised what was starting inside between his friends and the bikers from Ryka's.

What had started as a small scuffle broke out into full-scale war between the guys from Ryka's and everyone else.

Pepsi bottles and any missile that came to hand flew through the air.

Had the furniture not been bolted to the floor inside, the chairs and stools would have become a major problem. One guy wielded a motorcycle chain, whilst others put on knuckle dusters to maximise the damage with their fists.

"Bloody hell!" Jimmy shouted. He ducked a Pepsi bottle thrown in his direction. He yelled to Speedy, "We'd better sort this out!"

Jimmy and Speedy, joined by Jokerman, waded in. They didn't throw fists. They jerked the brawlers out of the fray by their collars, caught hold of an arm just as it raised to strike a blow and spun the guy around using his own momentum.

"Cut it out before the cops arrive!"

Jimmy yelled the warning over and over, trying to get through the collective red mist. They all had to duck punches as they pulled the embattled rivals apart. Once the fighters had been separated and they realised the main aim was to stop the fight, not to exacerbate the trouble, things calmed down and the discussions began. Who started it, and who was going to be blamed if the cops showed up? Angry pockets of bikers shouted across the room at each other, threatening more violence later. Speedy stood on one of the tables, arms up, appealing for quiet.

Within moments he had calmed the place. Bikers sat on the ground with blood dripping from their noses and other wounds. One guy leaned forward, spitting out blood and a couple of teeth. Bikers leaned on the bar, sat at the tables and waited, nursing their wounds.

The guy that started the whole thing had a severely broken nose.

He pointed at Turd.

"He started it! Look what he did to my nose."

Speedy jumped down from the table and cut his tirade short.

"Look, this is my manor. I know these guys from the Busy Bee well. If Turd did that, you must have deserved it. We come here for a boy's night out; we don't expect to get involved in a brawl. And these brawls often seem to happen when Ryka's lot turn up in large numbers."

A big guy known as Spider stood up. "We came for a good night out, too, but it seems that's not going to happen now. All of you from Ryka's, let's go back to Box Hill. If any of you from the Ace or the Bee drop by the Ryka's café, you'd better come mob-handed, ready for a fight."

With that, the Ryka's crew all got up to leave.

Jokerman stepped forward, momentarily blocking their path to the door. "No problem, Spider, and when we do visit Box Hill, you're mine. I'm not joking. Now piss off back to Surrey."

A derisory jeer went up as the guys from Ryka's, licking their wounds, left the café.

Jimmy turned to Speedy.

"Sorry about that, Speedy, but I know Turd wouldn't have started that scrap without a good reason. In the meantime, I think we should get out of here and let everything calm down. Race you to Brent and back?"

Speedy nodded. They ran from the café, leapt on their bikes, fired them up and shot out of the bike park onto the North Circular. When the rest of the guys realised where they were going, it was too late to join in the race, so most stayed behind and waited for their return, just to see who won. Some of the others decided that if the cops did turn up, their wounds and injuries would mark them out as being involved, so they left, too.

Speedy and Jimmy were both good riders. They sped along the North Circular, overtaking and undertaking cars, accelerating to speeds touching the ton. At the Brent roundabout, the widely agreed halfway point, they completed the turn with one knee almost touching the road as their bikes leaned into the sharp bend of the roundabout.

Heading back to the Ace, they were neck and neck. Jimmy slowed his pace by a fraction to allow Speedy the accolade of getting back to his home turf first. Speedy realised what he was doing and decided that it would be better if they arrived together, as a draw. Surely that had to be the best way to show a united front to the bikers eagerly waiting to see who would win. They roared into the bike park together, pulled up side by side and high-fived each other. The waiting bikers all cheered the result.

The rest of the evening went off without further trouble.

"Hey Jokerman, you're going to have to explain that fat lip to Gerry tomorrow night unless an ice pack works tonight," Jimmy was grinning.

Jokerman smiled knowingly. "Yeah, but I think my fat lip will go down quicker than the black eye you have, mate."

Jimmy touched his eye. "Ouch, I didn't realise," he said. "I wonder which one of those Ryka's boys got lucky and landed one on me?"

"I don't know, but I do know he was lucky that you were trying to break it all up rather than going in for the kill, or he'd have copped worse than that."

They both laughed, rounded up the gang and left the Ace to race back to the Busy Bee.

Busy Bee Café & Record Night

Wednesday 11th September 1963

The girls finished college and caught the bus home. Their day had once again been uninspiring; no hair to cut or shape, just endless lectures on scalp science, hair protection and general health and safety issues. Nonetheless, they both sank into their seats on the bus, lit up a cigarette and chatted excitedly about the evening to come.

After tea, clearing away and doing her chores, Judy went up to get ready. She wore slacks again for riding on the bike, although she thought that, at some stage, she would have to wear a skirt. She opted for a blouse with buttons up the front, stiletto heel shoes, her black anorak jacket and a red chiffon scarf. Judy explained to her mum and dad that she was going to Gerry's house again. She'd be back by 10.30pm at the latest. She was deliberately pushing the time back, hoping for some more kissing time.

She hurried to the Three Horseshoes. Full of anticipation, she rounded the corner to see two bikes. Jokerman had already picked up Gerry, and they were waiting by the green with Jimmy. She didn't care if she looked overly keen as she ran to Jimmy, flung her arms around him and kissed him hard.

"Woo, that's the kind of welcome I like!" whispered Jimmy as they parted.

He got on and kick-started his bike. Judy climbed on the back. She squeezed him tightly as they rounded the green. The two bikes headed off to the Busy Bee.

When they arrived, the bike park was almost full. Around 80 bikes parked up meant the café would be heaving inside. They pulled in, parked up and headed inside the café. As always, the air was heavy with cigarette smoke. On the jukebox, *The House of the Rising Sun* by the Animals had just started, and all the pinball machines were occupied. The place was packed.

As they got into the bright light, Judy noticed that Jimmy's right eye was badly bruised. Turning to Jokerman, she noticed he had a fat lip.

"No good asking you what happened for Jimmy to get a black eye, since you have a fat lip," she said. "I bet you've got your story straight between you."

"Woo, don't blame me," replied Jokerman. He turned his head away from Gerry, who had started making a closer examination of his lip now that Judy mentioned it.

"It's nothing," Jimmy said, raising his voice above the noise. "Just a little scrap at the Ace last night. We're all fine."

Judy scanned the café. She could see that others were bearing injuries from the so-called 'little scrap' at the Ace. Turd and Madman in particular both looked like they'd done ten rounds with Henry Cooper.

"Well, that looks sore, Jimmy. Are you sure you're OK?" Judy said, her hand lovingly brushing Jimmy's cheek.

"Don't fuss. We're big boys; we're OK." Jimmy took hold of her hand to remove it from his cheek. "It's record night, and that's far more exciting and dangerous than any little scrap at the Ace." Judy and Gerry glanced at each other. Judy leaned toward Gerry and whispered, "How can record night be dangerous? What are we missing here? I thought they'd be playing records."

"I don't know," Gerry said. Then her expression changed. Eyes wide, she continued, "Unless they're set on breaking a few records? You know, speed records—dangerous stuff like that?"

The girls looked at Jokerman and Jimmy with worried frowns.

"What's record night?" Gerry asked, concerned.

"You're probably right to worry, girls," Vicky stepped in, emphasising the word 'girls'. Then, quietly, so only Judy and Gerry heard, "You might not have a boyfriend once it's over, or even a lift home."

She laughed and pushed past Judy. Babs wasn't so subtle; she elbowed Gerry in the back as she barged past. Judy placed a hand on Gerry's arm to calm her down.

"Ignore them. They're jealous. Don't start a fight with them; they're not worth the trouble."

"It's very simple," explained Jokerman. "A biker selects a record on the jukebox and, as soon as he's pressed the buttons, he runs to his bike, which is already fired up and idling on the stand. If he's quick, he can be away before the needle sets down on the record.

He then races up to the Elstree Res roundabout and back. If he gets back inside the café before the record finishes, he wins."

Jimmy cut in. "The bloody House of the Rising Sun is banned, as it's four and a half minutes long. Ordinary records last about three minutes. We all put a tanner in the kitty. If someone wins, he gets the kitty.

It's rare that anyone manages it, as you need to be doing a ton most of the way round the circuit."

"It sounds dangerous to me," Gerry said, a bit shocked.

"It is, darling," smirked Vicky. "It's very dangerous. Only Jimmy and Jokerman have ever done it, and some don't come back."

Before Gerry could respond, Jimmy spoke again.

"Enough of this morbid talk! Who's up first?"

Madman stepped forward.
"Me, Jimmy. I'm feeling good about this; tonight's my turn to win."

Madman put a tanner in the kitty. His Matchless 650 cc was outside, ticking over on the stand. He went to the jukebox, put a coin in and selected A6, 'Can't Help Falling in Love' by Elvis Presley.

"A good choice," Jimmy said to Judy and Gerry. "That one's almost three minutes long."

The crowd parted, leaving a clear path to the door. As soon as he had pressed the A and the 6, Madman was off, running to the door and outside. A couple of the guys cheered him on: "Go on, Madman, get 'er done!" He leapt on his bike, leaned forward into the handlebars to push it off the stand and selected first gear, all in one slick, practised movement. He roared out of the bike park onto the A41. His back wheel skidded sideways momentarily, but he held his nerve, kept the accelerator on and pulled the bike back out of the skid with skill and expertise borne out of hours of riding and practice. The record began as he left the bike park. It was a cracking start to record night.

'Wise men say, only fools rush in, but I can't help falling in love with you,' sang Elvis.

People rushed out before the end of Elvis's record in anticipation of Madman's return. Turd had been dispatched at the start of the evening to check that all riders rounded the roundabout and didn't try to cheat. Madman did indeed make the roundabout. Speeding back to the café, he overtook traffic at speeds of over 100mph. The A41, a three-lane road where the middle lane was used for traffic to overtake in either direction, could be lethal.

The crowd outside heard Madman's Matchless returning before they caught sight of his lights. The jukebox was turned up to full volume, so the crowd outside could hear.

"For I can't help falling in love with you," Elvis finished slowly. The piano rang out the last three notes as Madman slammed on his brakes and skidded violently. He managed to keep control of the skid; using his outstretched right leg, he swung his bike into the bike park, flicked the side-stand down, leaped off his bike and ran for the café. Elvis finished almost 15 seconds before he got there.

"Damn!" Yelled Madman. "Fucking damn! I thought I had it this time."

Someone slapped him on the shoulder, "Good try, Madman!"

One after another, bikers set off on the dangerous, crazy pursuit of beating the record he had selected on the jukebox. Turd never entered record night, as his Indian Scout bike was not quick enough to be involved. Instead, he was always dispatched to the Elstree Res roundabout to make notes of all those who turned there, ensuring that nobody could cheat.

"Right, my turn!" Jokerman shouted above the din in the café. His Norton sat ticking over on its stand, close to the door of the café. He kissed Gerry on the cheek, ensuring that Vicky saw it, and whispered, "This one is for you."

"Be careful," Gerry replied with a nervous smile.

He flipped his tanner into the kitty, went to the jukebox, winked at Gerry and pressed B4. With that, he was gone, out of the door and onto his Norton. He was out on the road before the needle touched the record.

Dusty Springfield's voice rang out, "*I don't know what it is that makes me love you so; I only know I never want to let you go, cos you started something, and can't you see that ever since we met you had a hold on me. It happens to be true; I only want to be with you.*"

Gerry smiled. She caught Vicky's eye and mouthed the words, "He's mine now; watchagonna do about it?" Vicky gave Gerry a menacing snarl in return. Gerry knew she would end up in a fight with her at some stage.

The crowd left the café to watch for Jokerman. He took the roundabout with his knee down, accelerating away like a professional racer. Turd was impressed and thought Jokerman could do it this time, depending on what record he'd chosen.

Concentrating as though his life depended on it, Jokerman calculated the distance between an oncoming car overtaking in the middle lane. He could give up the chance of winning and play it safe, or he could take a chance on the overtaking car being that bit slow, giving him time to overtake the car he was fast-approaching. He wound open the accelerator, lowered his riding position further still and went for it. He narrowly missed the oncoming overtaking car. He jinked his bike left as he scraped through the space between the car he was overtaking and the oncoming car, with inches to spare. Horns from all three of the other cars blared as he left them behind him. He would think about what could have happened at some point later, probably when he retold the story.

Jokerman roared on through the dark. He screeched into the car park as Dusty Springfield finished with, "*No matter what you do, I only wanna be with you. I said, no matter, no matter what you do, I only want to be with you.*" He missed out by some 10 seconds.

Slightly disappointed but buzzing from his brush with three other vehicles and the adrenaline that the experience had brought, he spun around, took hold of Gerry and planted a long kiss on her lips.

"Chose the wrong song with the right words," he said. She almost melted with delight and kissed him back. Vicky and Babs watched the scene with what Gerry's dad would call 'faces like a slapped arse'—they were seething.

"Your turn, Jimmy!" Jokerman called out. "We're all counting on you to do it for the Busy Bee!"

Jimmy smiled. His bike was already primed, ticking over and ready for take-off.

He took Judy in his arms, kissed her and whispered in her ear, "Listen to the song."

She hugged him tight. He stepped up to the jukebox and selected C3. He was gone in a flash; his Triumph shot out onto the road outside the Busy Bee café.

The intro tune for the song started, then Billy Fury's voice rang out: "*A thousand stars in the skies, like the stars in your eyes, they say to me that there will never be no other love like yours for me.*" Judy went weak at the knees. She knew that Jimmy felt as strongly about her as she did about him.

Jimmy rode his bike like the wind. He rounded the roundabout, nodding to Turd as he leaned his bike low into the turn. Turd could only watch and admire Jimmy's skill. He knew that he could follow Jimmy back to the Busy Bee. Jimmy always rode last on record night.

Jimmy's selected tune played for just over 3 minutes. He skidded into the Busy Bee bike park to shouts of "Jimmy, Jimmy, Jimmy!" from the crowd. He kicked his bike onto the stand and ran into the open door of the café as Billy Fury sang, "*...tell me you're mine once more.*" The record finished. He pumped a fist into the air and yelled, "Yes!"

Judy ran over and jumped into Jimmy's arms, squealing with delight. Jimmy held her up as they kissed, and everyone hooted and cheered. Jokerman slapped Jimmy on the back, shouting,

"Come up for air, mate, that was some ride!"

Turd ran in.

"I've never seen anything like that, Jimmy! You took the roundabout at breakneck speed!"

Somebody had put Cliff Richard on the jukebox. 'Dynamite' started playing, and it summed the moment up to perfection.

"Blimey, it's almost 9.30," Jimmy said. "I must get you home. Come on, Jokerman, let's go."

Jimmy reached out for Judy's hand, and they left the Busy Bee, buzzing. Jokerman and Gerry took off to Radlett, whilst Jimmy and Judy rode to Letchmoreheath.

Once again, Jimmy stopped his bike just outside the village. He eased his bike onto the main stand, dismounted, and remounted to face Judy. There was a slight chill in the air because of the clear night sky. The stars shone brightly, and they gazed into each other's eyes, almost bursting with desire. As Jimmy leaned forward to kiss Judy, she put her finger on his lips.

"I'm not expected home until 10.30, so we have a bit more time tonight. There's a secluded bench behind the duck pond. It'll be very quiet down there," she whispered.

Jimmy freewheeled the bike down the hill, past the Three Horseshoes pub. They stopped by the duck pond, and he put the bike onto the centre stand. The ground was still firm from the summer, so the bike was stable. They made their way around the pond and sat on the secluded bench. Judy snuggled close to Jimmy. He put his arm around her shoulders and pulled her closer. Their lips met. The kisses were gentle at first, exploring boundaries and discovering what the other liked to do with their mouth, tongue, lips. Jimmy lifted Judy's chin, and his lips made their way down her neck and around to the front of her throat, where his teeth started nipping gently at her delicate, sensitive skin.

His fingers held her head still whilst he moved his mouth closer to her collarbone. He licked the skin there, and a fleeting thought of, "I'm so glad I didn't put scent on this evening," crossed her mind. She gave a giggle at the thought. Jimmy leaned back to look at her face, to check she wasn't laughing at something he was doing. She looked deep into his eyes, and he knew she wasn't laughing at him.

"Why did you stop?" she whispered. Jimmy said nothing. He kissed her again and unzipped her jacket, slipped his hands inside and started to undo the buttons of her blouse.

Once Jimmy felt the bare skin of her waist, he ran his hand up her back, giving her no time to protest—not that she was about to— and he expertly undid her bra. In one movement, he slid his hand to her front to caress her perfectly shaped, firm breast, gently squeezing her nipple. Judy drew in a sharp, excited breath. They were both breathing heavily with barely contained, raw passion.

Jimmy took hold of Judy's hand and directed it up the inside of his thigh. She pulled back, short of his crotch. He didn't force the issue but held her hand where it had got to. She could feel beneath the fabric of his jeans that he was hard; very, very hard.

"I'm sorry, Jimmy. Please don't make me go too far, too fast," she said.

He sucked in a breath, held it for a moment and let it out, like he was smoking a cigarette. Jimmy nodded and smiled at her. He noticed that his watch read 10.25, and, reluctantly, he let go of her hand and took his other hand from her blouse.

"Come on, angel, let's get you home before this gets out of hand and you're late getting home. Don't want your dad chasing me just yet. I'll pick you up on Friday. 7pm, same place. I've got night school tomorrow evening." He smiled, kissed her once more and watched her straighten her clothes.

Judy watched the back lights of Jimmy's bike as he rode off home. Then she skipped up the road and made it home for 10.30.

"Is that you, love?" her dad's voice called from the living room.

"Yes, Dad, home on time. I'm off to bed—goodnight."

From Russia with Love

Friday 13th September 1963

The girls met on the bus to Watford on their way to college for the last day of the week. Both drawing on their cigarettes, they discussed the fact that they had endured their first week at college. One week out of a three-year hairdressing course, and they had not so much as lifted a comb yet, let alone seen a head of hair. They giggled, reflecting that their love lives, however, had taken an enormous leap forward, all in the same week.

Gerry was besotted with Jokerman. He made every effort to keep her amused and constantly made her laugh, except on the occasions that they were preoccupied, usually when they were kissing wildly. She enjoyed the couple of drop-offs on the bike. They had almost gone too far in a bus shelter at Battlers Green after record night. Judy laughed when Gerry told her how it seemed that Jokerman had at least two pairs of hands, and they were all over her. Her resistance had been little more than a token wone, and she only managed to stop him when his hand eased inside the front of her slacks. That was a step too far for her.

"'Not so fast, cowboy,' I whispered in his ear, biting his ear lobe quite sharply. He got the message. I'm not sure how long I can keep up the resistance because we were made for each other," Gerry said, all starry-eyed.

The bus pulled up at Watford Station in the high street, and they made their way to college.

That evening after supper, Judy's dad asked, "Are you off out to Gerry's again tonight, love? That's three times this week."

"No, Dad, we're meeting up at St John's Youth Club in Radlett tonight. Friday night's mixed night and should be good fun," Judy said, thinking on her feet.

"I'll drive you over, love; can't have Gerry's dad doing all the taxi work, can we now?" Judy's dad said. "What time do you need to be there?"

A shiver went down Judy's spine. She hadn't thought this eventuality through.

"6.30pm at Gerry's house, please, Dad."

How was she going to get back to the Three Horseshoes to meet Jimmy? She knew Gerry was meeting Jokerman at 6.45pm, so if she could get Jokerman to ride over to Letchmore Heath, get Jimmy and bring him back to Radlett to get her, that might work.

"Better get moving, then. It's 6pm already," Dad said.

She changed quickly into a mohair jumper, a black pleated skirt, stockings, black stiletto-heeled shoes and her black plastic coat. Judy knocked on Gerry's front door, then turned and waved to her dad as he drove off.

Gerry's dad answered the door with surprise, "Hello, Judy. I wasn't expecting you; I'll call Gerry down."

Gerry ran down the stairs, a little shocked to see Judy standing there looking worried. "Hi Judy, come on up. I'm nearly ready," she said, as if it was all pre-arranged.

Upstairs, Judy revealed the dilemma that she had had to let her dad drive her over or risk giving away that she had other plans. Gerry finished dressing, grabbed her coat, yelled goodbye to her mum and dad and pulled the door closed behind them. They ran out towards Malone's, where Gerry had arranged to meet Jokerman. Once he turned up and they had explained it all, Jokerman nodded.

"Wait here. I won't be long." He sped off, up Battlers Green Drive, then left onto New Road towards Letchmore Heath.

Fifteen minutes later, they heard the unmistakable roar of two bikes approaching. Judy let out a sigh of relief.

As they pulled up, Jimmy winked at Judy.

"All OK at home, I hope?" he said.

Judy nodded and climbed onto the back of his bike. "OK, off to the Busy Bee to make arrangements for this weekend. Then I thought we could go to the Odeon in St Albans—they have _From Russia with Love_, the new Bond film, on at 7.45.

We'll get you girls back by 10.30. Is that OK?"

Both girls nodded, Jokerman winked, and they set off down Willow Way, left on the Watford Road towards the Busy Bee.

When they arrived, the café was packed. The jukebox was playing *Sweets for My Sweet* by the Searchers. Madman and Turd were in the middle of an arm wrestle, with lighted candles on each side, to burn the loser's hand. A crowd gathered round, cheering them on as money changed hands, betting on the outcome. With a twinkle in his eye and one final grimace, Turd put all his might into his last effort. Madman caved in with a shout and extinguished the candle with his hand. Turd punched the air, laughing.

"Who's next?" he asked.

Jimmy stepped in.

"Not so fast, Turd. I just want a moment to talk about Sunday," he shouted above the music.

People stopped talking. "I thought we could take a ride out to Southend on Sunday before the last of the summer weather disappears. There are dodgems, amusement arcades, the pier, ten-pin bowling and fish and chips. What do you say?" he asked.

Lots of nods and sounds of agreement came from the gang, and Jimmy took it that they were all in.

"OK. 10am, meet here in the bike park, grab a coffee and maybe a bite to eat, and we'll leave at 10.30am sharp," he announced. "See you on Sunday."

Jimmy turned and grabbed Judy's hand. They left the café, followed by Jokerman and Gerry.

The two bikers and their girls left the Busy Bee and made their way north, then across to St Albans. They pulled up in London Road, parked up outside the Odeon and bought tickets for the film. They made their way to the back row in the far corner of the circle and settled down to watch the latest Bond film.

It didn't take long before attention turned from the film toward each other, and the snogging started. Both couples missed most of the film, stopping only for the occasional fag, with their feet on the back of the seat in front, blowing plumes of smoke into the darkness of the cinema.

After the film ended, they adjusted their clothing for decency's sake and left the theatre separately. Jokerman headed to Radlett, and Jimmy rode via Bricket Wood to the A41, then on to Letchmore Heath via Patchetts Green. When they got back, he remembered the secluded bench at the duck pond, switched off the engine and coasted to a halt. "How long have we got, angel? It's just after 10."

"Just under half an hour. I said I'd be home by 10.30," Judy said as she got off the bike and made her way to the bench.

They carried on where they'd left off in the cinema, content in each other's arms, lips constantly locked. Jimmy had noticed that Judy was wearing a skirt. It wasn't long before his hand found her knee and started slowly edging up her thigh. She shivered with delight, ignoring the progress for the moment. His hand reached the top of the stocking where it connected to the suspender belt. His hand felt the bare skin of her thigh, and he gave a deep, shuddering sigh of desire.

Judy took in a deep breath, leaned forward and kissed him as hard as she could. Jimmy took the kiss as a positive signal and edged his hand further up her leg. His thumb felt the seam of her knickers and tracked the stitching back and forth. Judy hesitantly placed her hand on the front of his jeans. She didn't know what to expect.

She and Gerry had giggled about it all on the bus, at break times and after college, but neither really knew what would happen when they finally got into the situation of intimacy. It was all guesswork and speculation—until suddenly, it wasn't.

Jimmy started fidgeting, pressing his groin into Judy's hand. Encouraged by the rhythm and the pressure, she started to carefully move the palm of her hand in gentle opposition to his movements. Jimmy's excitement became more vocal, and a deep, guttural moan began behind the kisses. He let out a gasp and shuddered under her hand. He withdrew his hand from Judy's groin a moment before Judy intended it to stop.

"Oh, fuck…" he said. "I'm… wow, that was intense." He couldn't look her in the eyes, and she detected a hint of embarrassment. She put her hands on either side of his face and kissed his lips gently. "We need to find somewhere more comfortable in the future," she suggested.

He nodded. "My mum is off to Ireland in a couple of weeks. Maybe we can have a night in together at my house then?"

Judy took a deep breath and nodded. They made their way back to the bike and enjoyed one last kiss. "Thank you for being you; you're amazing. I'll pick you up here on Sunday at 9.45am."

"Better not. My dad's getting suspicious. I'll be at Gerry's on Sunday morning, so you and Jokerman can pick us up at Malone's at 9.45am."

Judy scurried off home. She turned around to blow a kiss as she went.

Saturday 14th September 1963

Judy packed an overnight bag. When her dad dropped her off at Bishop's supermarket on Saturday morning for work, she kissed him on the cheek. "Thanks, Dad, I can walk to Gerry's after work tonight. I'll be back tomorrow around 7pm. I'll get a lift, and there'll be no need to keep dinner hot for me."

"OK, love, don't stay out late in Watford tonight. We'll see you tomorrow. Have a good time," he said. He left thinking about how grown-up his daughter had become in such a short time after leaving school.

The girls didn't go out into Watford that evening. Instead, they went for a long walk and talked about Judy's experience on the bench down by the pond. Though they giggled a lot, they also realised something had changed. The relationship was more real and more grown-up. It seemed like they had suddenly walked from one room to another, leaving childhood experiences behind them and walking forward toward unknown, more grown-up and serious experiences.

"What do I do now? When we eventually go to his house, I think he'll be expecting... you know..." Judy said. "Would it be OK to stop him before he... we go too far?"

"I don't know," replied Gerry, equally concerned. "I think Jokerman is going to be expecting the same. I bet he and Jimmy have been talking about... the bench experience as much as we are."

"Have you ever... you know... done it?" asked Judy.

"You know I haven't!" responded Gerry. "I'd have told you, just like you've told me. We're best friends. That's what best friends do."

Southend on Sea Ride Out

Sunday 15th September 1963

Full of excitement for the ride to Southend, the girls woke early on Sunday morning. They dressed appropriately in slacks, mohair jumpers, anorak jackets and chiffon scarves to protect their beehive hairstyles. Gerry told her parents they were spending the day with an old school friend in Bushey.

The girls made their way to Malone's, where Jimmy and Jokerman were already waiting. Judy nudged Gerry when they spotted the guys.

"They're eager, aren't they?"

"Course they are. We're the best thing that's happened to them," replied Gerry smugly.

The motorbikes glistened in the bright, early autumn sun. Dew on the grass and a clear blue sky overhead promised a perfect day for a ride out to the seaside.

"Morning, girls. Ready for a day by the sea?" said Jokerman.

The girls nodded, kissed their respective guys and climbed on board the motorbikes.

They weren't the first to arrive at the Busy Bee, but they'd be the first to leave, which was just the way Jimmy liked it.

A few of the others he expected to be there were already tucking into a quick breakfast or holding a cup of coffee. They ordered a mug of coffee each and stood around in the bike park area, waiting for stragglers and the usual latecomers.

"I should have told Turd we were meeting at 9:30, not 10," said Jimmy. "He's always late."

"Yeah, well, you told him we're leaving at 10:30, so if he's not here, he'll just have to catch us up, if he can," replied Jokerman.

"Madman's here. He's just turned up, so Turd won't be far behind," responded Jimmy.

Madman pulled in and parked his bike.

"Turd was having a problem with his bike. It wouldn't start, so I offered him a ride on the back of mine, but he said if he's not here by the time we leave, he'll either catch us up or see us in the week."

"That bloody bike," crowed Jokerman. "Oh, listen, it sounds like he got it started."

Another bike turned up, and Jokerman was proven right. Turd had managed to get his bike going.

By 10.15am, there were already 16 bikes for the Southend ride-out. All the usual gang were there, and joining Turd, Madman, Bumper and Grumpy were a few other regulars. Two new riders rode in, one on a Triumph Bonneville, the other on a Norton Dominator. On the back of the bikes were Vicky and Babs. They pulled up and dismounted.

One of the guys walked over to Jimmy and Jokerman.

"Which one of you is Jimmy?" he said. "I'm Keith, and this is John. We're from Edgware. We met Vicky and Babs last night, and they thought we could tag along to Southend today."

"Yeah, no problem. The more, the merrier," welcomed Jimmy.

By 10.30, there were more than 30 bikes ready to set off for a day out at Southend. It was around 59 miles to Southend-on-Sea. An easy run.

"OK, listen up," Jimmy raised his voice to get everyone's attention. "We'll pick up the North Circular just north of Barnet, then head on to the A13 at Dagenham and straight on to Southend. If we get separated, we'll meet in front of the pier. We'll wait for 15 minutes to give everyone the chance to catch up, and then we'll be off, OK? Staggered column, command the road, try and stick together. Turd, you and Bumper bring up the rear, please. Ride ahead to let us know if anyone has to drop out. Enjoy the ride."

With that, Jimmy kick-started his machine and led the pack out onto the A41 towards Barnet. As they left, Gerry caught Vicky's eye and mouthed, "Not bad, but he's mine." She grinned and pointed at Jokerman's back. Vicky's mouth curled in a snarl.

She mouthed, "Fuck off, you bitch."

The bikes roared out of the Busy Bee bike park.

The journey took a little more than an hour. They arrived in Southend just before noon and parked up as close to the pier as they could.

There were still plenty of visitors at the seaside resort, despite it being after the school holidays. The scent of fish and chips, vinegar and candyfloss hung in the air. Noise of the funfair came at them in waves. Shrieks and screams from the rollercoaster and laughter and friendly yelling as cars collided at the dodgems mixed with the sound of waves gently rolling up the beach.

It was still warm enough for people to be sitting on the beach with colourful windbreaks dotted along the shore, as far as the eye could see.

"Right, who's up for it?" said Jimmy. "A walk along the pier, dodgems, fish and chips and ten-pin bowling. Then we'll leave around 4pm?"

The throng of bikers gathered round after parking up their bikes. A murmur of "Yeah, sounds good," and "Catch you later," went up, and the group made their way to the front of the pier to tag along or disperse as they pleased.

Entrance to the pier to walk cost sixpence, and to walk and ride the train cost a shilling. The pier was more than a mile long, but that was nothing to a gang of teenage bikers who could lark around as they made their way to the end. The couples in the group held hands as they strolled along, kissing every now and then. The younger, single lads, affected by the sea air, played leapfrog just to see if they could keep it up for the whole mile.

The gang fell about laughing when Turd collapsed under Madman's weight. They both tumbled to the wooden planks of the walkway, with the swirling waves around the steel columns supporting the pier visible through the cracks.

"Blimey, Turd, we've only just started. Best you just do leaps all the way if this is what's going to happen," said Madman, and they rolled about laughing.

By the time they reached the end of the pier, the wind had picked up and was stronger than at the shoreline. White foam tipped the waves as they rolled through the steel structure of the pier. They leaned trustingly against the iron railing, the only thing preventing them from falling into the sea. Some of the lads sat on the railing, tempting fate, daring each other. Everyone smoked, sending plumes of white into the fresh air and buffeting breeze.

Jokerman and Jimmy shared a match to light their cigarettes under the onslaught of a determined sea breeze and were concentrating on the task at hand, not on the girls, for a moment.

Vicky and her new fella strolled past, arm in arm, seemingly love's young dream.

"I'll get him back one day, you slag," Vicky whispered as they passed Gerry, who stood alone for the moment.

Jokerman looked up in time to see Gerry launch herself at Vicky.

"Over my dead body, you ugly cow!"

"What's going on?" said Jimmy.

"No idea. I think Vicky must have said something to Gerry," replied Jokerman.

"Are you going to do something?" asked Jimmy.

"I wouldn't try to get in the middle of that catfight if I were you," cut in Madman. He took a step backwards, out of the way of the two girls.

The newcomers, John and Keith, stood on the other side of the scrapping girls. John held Keith back from trying to separate them. After a bit of hair-pulling, where both Gerry and Vicky ended up in a stalemate, neither able to let go for fear of the other getting a better grip, Jokerman and Keith managed to take hold and pull the girls apart. Vicky had a few wisps of hair in her fist, but Gerry had a lot of hair in her hand. Gerry looked at the hair and threw it to the ground in disgust.

"Oh, that feels like I just scalped a horse," laughed Gerry.

Vicky broke away from Keith and lunged at Gerry. She tried to grab fistfuls of her hair again, but Gerry was ready for her. Gerry knocked Vicky to the ground. Gerry, hailing from a family with strong Scottish heritage, leapt on top of Vicky and started punching and slapping her about the face. She got a handful of hair on both sides of Vicky's head and started bashing her head onto the planks beneath them before Keith grabbed hold of Gerry and manhandled her off his girlfriend. Gerry fought back against Keith, and he had to let her go. He shoved her towards Jokerman.

"Get your bitch under control," he snarled.

"Cut it out, you two," said Jimmy. "We're here for a nice day out." He stepped between Keith and Jokerman, but Keith had decided to square up to his love rival.

Jokerman gritted his teeth and snarled, "Don't even think about it, pal, cos you'll end up in the fucking sea."

Keith thought better of it, grabbed Vicky's hand and nodded to John, who grabbed Babs' hand. The four of them headed back down the pier.

"You OK, Gerry?" asked Judy.

"Yeah, I gave that cow what-for," Gerry replied.

"Well, she's been spoiling for a fight since that first night at the Bee," said Judy.

Jokerman turned to Gerry and held her hand.

"Now, listen to me, honey. I've only got eyes for you. No more fighting, OK? You don't need to. I'm yours."

Gerry looked up at Jokerman and nodded, then she nestled her head into his chest and allowed him to hug her tight.

The rest of the day was nothing but fun and filled with laughter. They took over the dodgems for a couple of rounds—no one else wanted to have a go while the lads were playing a bit too rough. Bumper lived up to his nickname and emerged victorious. They sat on the sand and ate fabulous fish and chips from newspapers using wooden forks and, finally, ended the day playing ten-pin bowling, which went off without a hitch—just a lot of fist pumps when the odd strike was achieved.

They rode back towards the Busy Bee. Some veered off and made their way home before they got there. Jimmy sat at the Busy Bee bike park and made sure everyone was accounted for before setting off to drop Judy off at Gerry's house. Judy needed to fetch her overnight bag, then get back to Letchmore Heath by 7pm. Jimmy wanted to take her home, but Judy insisted that she'd get a lift from Gerry's dad to protect their deception.

Moving up a gear

Friday 27th September 1963

Judy and Gerry finished their third week at Casio College, their first full week of hairdressing practical stuff. They knew it was just the beginning of three years' worth of hard work ahead. Judy was determined to learn as much about the business side of hairdressing as possible to help her to open her own salon one day.

Once on the bus home, they went upstairs, lit up a cigarette and sat back to plan the weekend ahead. The past few weeks had been great fun, with visits to the Busy Bee to play pinball, listen to the latest songs and, on record night, to cheer the guys on as they tried to beat the music on their bikes. Only Jimmy had managed it so far. Neither Vicky nor Babs had been seen at the Busy Bee since the Sunday in Southend. Nobody missed them. At the end of each night out, the two friends enjoyed increasingly more intimate moments with their guys.

The upcoming weekend was going to be a different ballgame. They made their plans on the bus ride from college. They decided they'd be back by 10pm after visiting the Busy Bee. Then, the story was that on Saturday night, they were going to stay with their friend in Bushey.

Judy would take an overnight bag with her to work at her Saturday job, and afterwards, she would go to Gerry's to change. They would then leave together, with a promise to be back by 7pm on Sunday.

Their excitement was uncontainable at the thought of staying at Jimmy's house. His mother had gone to Ireland and wasn't expected back until Monday evening. No more bus shelters, uncomfortable secluded benches, or squeezing up on the bike. The weekend promised comfort and romance all the way. They leaned their heads back, drew on their cigarettes and blew smoke into the air with self-satisfied grins.

Saturday 28th September 1963

Judy's dad dropped her off at her Saturday job at 7.45am. She was working on the delicatessen counter and needed to set up before opening at 9. She had a change of clothing in her overnight bag.

"Thanks, Dad, I'll be home by 7 tomorrow night," she said as she got out of the car.

"OK, love, enjoy yourself, and don't stay up too late tonight."

The day seemed to drag on forever. Judy found it difficult to concentrate, her mind elsewhere.

"I asked for a quarter of ox tongue, not brawn!" one angry customer pointed out.

She had a constant fluttering of butterflies in her stomach.

She was filled with a mixture of excitement, nervousness and the feeling that she was about to enter new territory that night. The anticipation was overwhelming. She struggled through the day.

"Are you alright, Judy?" Chris, the manager of the meat department, asked as he passed her counter on his way for a tea break. "You don't seem yourself today, love."

"Oh, I'm fine, thanks, Chris. I have a big night out tonight, that's all." She stunned herself, even as the words came out of her mouth. 'What the hell am I saying that for?' she thought.

"Have fun, love, and don't do anything I wouldn't do," he said with a grin and a wink. "That gives you plenty of scope."

Judy felt her face go red. She looked down and responded, "Thanks, Chris, I'll bear that in mind."

Chris laughed loudly as he went to the staff room with his malt loaf, pint of milk and playing cards for a quick game of crib with the butcher's Saturday boy, who was learning the game.

At last, after closing at 5pm, Judy walked towards Gerry's house, up the hill, through Scrubbit's Square, past the recreation ground and on to Willow Way. Gerry opened the door to her knock, and they ran upstairs to change. Both girls were so excited, but then Gerry brought their exuberant mood down to earth a little.

"Do you think our small bags will be OK on the bikes?" Judy thought for a second. "Yes, I think so. Don't worry; we'll sort it out somehow."

They nodded to each other, let out an excited giggle, then finished putting on their makeup.

They had arranged to meet the guys at Malone's at 6.30pm. They said goodbye to Gerry's mum and dad, then almost ran around the corner to where the guys were waiting. After a quick kiss, the girls jumped on the back of their respective boyfriends' bike with their overnight bags securely trapped between their fronts and the guys' backs. They set off to Bushey, and Jimmy's house, bursting with anticipation of what the night ahead would bring.

Jimmy was an only child. He lived with his mum in a council house in South Oxhey, which was not a great side of town. The girls came from families that, whilst they were by no means wealthy, neither did they live on or close to the 'breadline'—the line where 'making do' meets poverty.

When they arrived at Jimmy's mum's house, the girls stood at the front, on the pavement, and looked up and down the street. Though Jimmy's house was one of the better ones, none of the buildings were much to shout about. In the middle of a long row of terraced houses, the house where Jimmy lived needed a bit of a touch-up with paint and maybe new window and door frames, but the curtains were clean, and unlike some of the other houses, the curtains at least opened—and indeed, were proper curtains, not sheets or blankets tacked to the window.

Jokerman saw the girls' expressions and before Jimmy saw them. He shook them out of their dismay.

"Look, wipe that look off your face before Jimmy sees it. Jimmy's dad was in the army. He was killed in the war, fighting in France. Jimmy never knew his dad. He was born after his dad was killed, blown apart from stepping on a land mine in France," Jokerman said in a hushed voice.

"His mum's done a good job raising Jimmy on her own, so keep your thoughts to yourself, OK?"

They parked up in the front garden of Jimmy's house. Jimmy unlocked the front door and ushered the girls in ahead of him and Jokerman. The girls stood around in the hallway, unsure of where they should go.

"This is the way to the kitchen," said Jokerman. "Shall I put the kettle on?"

Jimmy was very excited; he'd bought the latest single from a new group called The Beatles. The song was called 'She Loves You'. He put it on the record player in the middle room between the front room and the kitchen. Then he turned to Judy and said,

"I hope this is true," as The Beatles sang: *"She loves you, yeah, yeah, yeah."*

Judy playfully punched his chest. She smiled up at him, and he wrapped his arms around her in an embrace, completely ignoring Gerry and Jokerman as they swayed to the music.

"Come on, Gerry, let's leave them to it. They don't look like they're coming up for air any time soon," said Jokerman, leading Gerry by the hand towards the staircase.
"I stay here quite often and almost have my own room. Jimmy's mum has problems with sleeping, and she stays downstairs in the front room where the telly is."

They made their way upstairs, kissing as they went.

The Beatles were set on repeat mode; 'She Loves You' played in a constant loop. He gently eased her onto the sofa. Then he whispered in her ear,

"Why don't we get comfortable upstairs? I have a very large bed."

Judy nodded shyly. Jimmy pulled her from the sofa and led her up the stairs. Jimmy opened his bedroom door and led her inside. From the room next to theirs, noises of delight and passion could be heard above the record on repeat downstairs.

"Jokerman and Gerry are obviously enjoying themselves," said Jimmy, then bent his head to Judy's neck and nipped at her earlobe, making her sigh.

Jimmy's jacket hit the floor, his T-shirt slipped over his head, he pulled Judy's mohair jumper over her head and released the clasp of her bra all in one movement. Her breasts pressed firm against his bare chest.

They lay on the bed. Jimmy expertly pushed down Judy's slacks, leaving her legs bare to the slight chill of the room. Naked apart from her knickers, she shuddered as cool air brought her skin into goosebumps. Jimmy thought how beautiful she looked. He started to remove his jeans. They kissed gently at first, then more firmly as he became more and more excited.

Jimmy straddled Judy's legs and ran his hands up her thighs. Gently, he pulled down her knickers to her knees. She gasped. Somehow, he moved his leg off hers so he could slip down her knickers and take them off her legs, then he started kissing her waist, around the sides, where the delicate, sensitive area lay.

She didn't know whether to laugh or squeal with delight as his teeth nipped gently around her navel and he started moving down her belly with his teeth and tongue. He deliberately avoided her breasts and pubic area, and by the time he had finished removing her clothes, she couldn't think straight.

His hand finally went toward her crotch and gently caressed her mound. His fingers flickered across her clitoris, a feather-light touch, and she moaned aloud, head back, eyes closed.

She slipped her hand inside his underpants and clasped his stiff penis. She was surprised by how big it was, although she had nothing to judge it by, as it was the first penis she had ever touched.

Jimmy gasped and had to stop what he was doing. They parted, reluctantly, so he could slip off his own pants.

Judy whispered, "Be gentle, my darling. This is my first time." Then, as an afterthought, she said, "Have you got any johnnies?"

Jimmy nodded. His voice also came out in a whisper, "I'll protect you. I've got a full packet; it's my first time, too!"

The confession took Judy by surprise. She thought he would have had lots of experience. The news brought forth a warm feeling throughout her body. She thought it would be so very easy to fall completely in love with him.

Judy watched, fascinated, as Jimmy rolled a johnnie onto his erect penis. As gently as he could, he fumbled around and eventually was able to enter Judy slowly, gently, frightened that he would hurt her at first. She gasped and bit her bottom lip as the fleeting yet sharp pain took her breath. They found their rhythm and moved in unison. Slowly to begin with, then faster and ultimately, harder.

They lay in each other's arms, dozing and snuggling. Then the kissing started to become more passionate again. After a little while, their bodies recovered from their exertions, and they started over again.

By the third time, they were exhausted. Jimmy lit a cigarette, and they shared it. After a minute or two, Jimmy looked down to remove the johnnie. He was horrified to see it had split from the multiple times it had been used. He removed it and reached for a fresh one in anticipation of a long night. He decided not to tell Judy that the johnnie had split.

They continued on and on, satisfying each other in every way they could imagine. Jimmy used another two johnnies, leaving only two remaining. Eventually, totally exhausted but very satisfied with each other, they fell asleep, wrapped in satisfied bliss.

Sunday 29th September 1963

Jimmy woke at around 6am. He went downstairs and returned with two cups of tea. There was no sign of life from the room next door. Gerry and Jokerman were still fast asleep after an energetic night of bedroom gymnastics.

Jimmy put one mug of tea down on the bedside table next to Judy and sat staring at her in amazement.

"You are the most wonderful thing that's ever happened to me, angel," he whispered. He studied her sleeping form for a moment more, then leaned forward to kiss her forehead.

Judy stirred and started waking up. She smiled a delicious smile, stretched like a lithe cat and muttered, "Get back into bed, my gorgeous biker." Jimmy slid between the covers.

Judy snuggled close to him.

"Ooh, you're cold," she said. "I think I know just the thing to warm you up."

Judy's hand traced its way down his chest, across the smattering of chest hair, along his flat stomach and down. Her fingertips teased his senses. He gasped, as he thought her hand was close to touching him where he wanted her to touch, but at the last moment, her fingers veered away. It was almost as though she knew what she was doing. After a couple of times, he put his hand under the covers, found her wrist, grasped it and firmly guided her hand to the place she couldn't quite seem to find before. She giggled at his frustration but then took it all a bit more seriously and worked her hand up the length of his erection in smooth, delicate movements.

He put his hand on hers again, to stop her. She looked up at him with a slight frown. "Am I doing it wrong?" she asked.

"No, you're doing it just right, and that's the problem."

Jimmy reached for one of the two remaining johnnies. He passed the small, sealed package to Judy and she split the cellophane open.

She had watched him perform the exercise before, and she gently rolled the johnny onto Jimmy's very stiff penis. She pushed the bed sheets down and off the bottom of the bed and watched as his penis bobbed gently at her every touch. She kissed the tops of his thighs and watched the reaction. His balls tightened up every time his penis moved off his groin, and she was fascinated. Satisfied that she had the full attention of Jimmy's erect penis, she climbed onto his stomach. She sat upright and gently manoeuvred herself so that he slid inside of her with only a little guidance. He gasped as she rolled her hips back and forth, arching her back, throwing her head backwards. His hands went to her hips and her movements became more vigorous, moving her hips faster. Jimmy pulled her to him, close to his chest, and he rolled them both over in one movement. With Judy on her back, Jimmy hooked one arm under her leg, then hooked the other arm under her other leg and stretched her legs to enhance the sensations. Try as he might, he couldn't last much longer, but he made sure he felt the start of her orgasm before he lost concentration and his own began. With shaking limbs, he let loose one leg, then the other, and lowered himself onto the bed next to Judy. Her eyes were closed, and her cheeks, throat and collarbones were visibly flushed in a pretty, pink hue. He kissed her throat, just where the indentation started. She sighed and ran her fingers through his hair.

Jimmy lit up two cigarettes and passed one to Judy. The mugs of tea stood ignored and cold on the bedside tables. They dozed for a while, Jimmy on his back, his arm tucked under Judy, holding her close. She dozed in the crook between his shoulder and his arm, safe, secure and blissfully happy.

When Judy's eyes flickered open, the morning sunshine hadn't moved very far, so she knew they'd not been asleep very long. Jimmy smiled down at her, then looked at the one remaining unopened johnnie, winked at her and, without a word, set about putting the contraceptive to good use.

At 10am Judy woke up, exhausted but basking in an afterglow of fulfilment. Jimmy got up and went downstairs to make breakfast for them both. He came into the room with a bacon sandwich and a fresh mug of tea for her.

"Gerry and Jokerman are up and dressed, angel," he said. "Sounds like they had a great night together, too."

Judy scoffed down her bacon sandwich like she'd not eaten for a week. She wiped her greasy fingers on the tea towel Jimmy offered her and brushed breadcrumbs out of the bed onto it.

"Can I take a quick bath before we get dressed and take off for the day? You can scrub my back, if you want," she teased.

"Sure," Jimmy said with a grin. "But don't get me too excited— we're out of johnnies."

They all helped to tidy up after themselves, taking longer than it should have, because they kept getting distracted by each other. The guys got their bikes ready for the ride out to Dunstable Downs, where they spent the rest of the day enjoying the fine weather, the scenery and the idea of falling a little in love. They found a roadside café and enjoyed a Pepsi and a hot dog for lunch, watching the world go by and getting to know each other better.

After another exciting ride, they made their way back to Radlett, arriving close to Gerry's house for 6.30pm. Though they were all tired out from hardly any sleep the night before combined with a hectic day, they reluctantly parted ways, promising to meet on Wednesday for record night at the Busy Bee. Jimmy and Jokerman arranged to pick them up at 7pm at the usual places.

Gerry's dad drove Judy home.

Judy called out, "Hello, I'm back! We had a really hectic day, so I'm going straight to bed. I'm tired out."

She went upstairs, dropped her bag on the floor and flopped onto her bed, exhausted but very pleased with herself.

Found Out

Wednesday 16th October 1963

A little more than two weeks after the exciting weekend at Jimmy's house, the secluded bench was back in use. They had had an uneventful two weeks, the relative tedium of work and college broken only by regular nights out at the Busy Bee Café. Jimmy and Judy were becoming increasingly exasperated. The fact that their only option was the bench down by the pond, which didn't allow any basic comfort or privacy, let alone any opportunity for real passionate lovemaking, frayed their tempers and increased their frustration. The sense of 'something missing' increased daily, it seemed, especially when they thought back and recalled the total freedom and intimacy they had enjoyed during that eventful weekend. They both longed for those few blissful hours they'd shared when Jimmy's mum was away, and they had had the security and comfort of a house in which to explore their newly released sexuality.

Possibly because of the sexual tension spilling over into her home life, Judy's mood changed. She sometimes became annoyed when she was tired from a day at college but still had her usual chores to complete.

"Yes, all right, Mum, I'll do the dishes later! I'm just having a sit-down. I've been on my feet all day!"

"That's all right, love, I'll do them," her mum replied and got up to do one more of Judy's chores.

Because of their daughter's bad moods, Judy's parents were becoming increasingly worried. Her dad, especially, grew increasingly suspicious of Judy's activities.

"She's always going out these days," he said to his wife. "I know she was always close to Gerry, but they've never been in each other's pockets like this, not even at school. It's becoming a regular thing. She never asks me to take her over to Gerry's, and Gerry never visits here these days."

He sat and thought about everything that had changed since Judy started college, and he decided things just didn't add up. That was when he decided that one evening, he would follow Judy the next time she was supposedly going to Gerry's house.

"Perhaps you should leave it, love," Judy's mum said as he prepared to play detective.

"And have her talking to you like she has been doing?" he replied. "Not on your life. I'll find out what she's playing at, why she's always in a bad mood when she comes home from college and why she's always exhausted and doesn't want to talk to us like she used to."

"She's a teenager. Of course she's changing! What normal young woman wants to sit at home every evening watching the same television programmes as her parents?" Judy's mum spoke in a low voice, so her husband had no real chance of hearing her. Not that he'd take any notice of her opinion if he did hear. Once he made up his mind, there was little anyone could say to change it, especially if the voice of reason was a female voice.

Up in her bedroom, Judy busied herself getting ready. Her mood buoyant, she fizzed with excitement at the prospect of seeing Jimmy. Judy frowned at her reflection as she applied her lipstick. Although it had only been two weeks ago, she longed for the opportunity to be with Jimmy in his bed or her bed—any bed would be better than the bench. But her longing was tempered by the fact that her period was late—more than a week late. Being late by even a few days had never happened before. She had been as regular as clockwork since her periods had settled down five years ago.

She stared at herself in the mirror, trying to look deep into her own eyes. The only thing she could come up with was that it might have something to do with her emotions; the way her body reacted to Jimmy was an indication that the usual way her mind worked was out of whack and all over the place. Surely it could account for her bodily functions, too?

Perhaps her period was just late, and maybe it would catch up soon. A smile flicked across her face. She almost believed herself. The frown returned as her mind played devil's advocate and considered that, on the other hand, if the unthinkable was to have happened, and she was pregnant after just a few hours of passion, it would serve her right for being so free and easy with Jimmy.

With a supreme effort, she pulled that unimaginable scenario to the back of her mind and finished getting ready. Judy ran downstairs, calling out to her mum and dad as she went.

"I'll be home by 10.30. Bye!"

She closed the front door behind her and walked quickly past the front of the house. Dad's car wasn't there. It was unusual, but she thought nothing of it.

Judy skipped down to the corner, and as soon as she saw Jimmy by the green, she ran the rest of the way. She looked both ways as she crossed the road and threw her arms around him, taking him by surprise. Judy kissed him harder than she had before.

"Wow!" said Jimmy when she allowed him to come up for air. She laughed and climbed on the back of the bike.

"Whatever brought that on, let's have some more," he chuckled. Jimmy kick-started the bike, and they set off around the green towards Elstree and the Busy Bee via the A41.

Judy's dad watched from the corner before the Three Horseshoes. He sat in his car, parked just off the road and out of their line of sight, but with a clear view of the pair as they greeted each other and then left on the motorbike. He was saddened when he saw Judy climb onto the bike, more because it confirmed his fears that she had been lying about where she was going. He sighed and set off in pursuit of his daughter and whoever was riding that bike. He managed to keep a safe distance behind them. With his thoughts in a whirl, he followed them into Dagger Lane, past Elstree Aerodrome, then onto the A41. He had tears in his eyes, troubled by her deceit but concerned that she was riding on the back of a motorbike without wearing a crash helmet.

Jimmy and Judy rode into the Busy Bee bike park. Jimmy slowed down and concentrated on looking for a prime location to park. Neither of them noticed the car that drove in behind them. As

Judy dismounted, she turned and saw her dad getting out of his car. Jack McDermott's face was red with rage, and she couldn't remember when she had ever seen him looking so angry. She watched, her mouth open and eyes wide, looking on in shock. He strode towards them, his arm waving towards Jimmy.

"What the hell are you doing on a motorbike with no crash helmet? And who the fuck is that guy? Yes, you; I'm talking about you, you cheeky bleeder!" Judy looked around and watched Jimmy's reaction to her dad's aggression. Jimmy blinked rapidly as he tried to process the reason behind the unprovoked verbal assault.

He would usually have given as good as he got with any other biker giving him grief, but the man striding towards him was old enough to be his dad, and his instinct was to be more subdued, even a little respectful of the man's age.

Judy had never heard her dad swear before. She was frozen to the spot. Tears pricked at her eyes in the embarrassment of it all. Jimmy had gotten off his bike and he stepped in front of Judy, blocking the strange man's path. He put up his hands to ward the man off.

"Calm down, sir; you seem upset. We don't want you having a heart attack."

"Heart attack! Who the fuck do you think you are? I'll damn well give you what for right now!"

Then he stopped, sensing that his verbal attack had got the attention of the bikers in the area, and they were starting to gather around the three of them.

"Judy, get in the car right now. I'll deal with you when we get home!" Jack snarled at his daughter.

Judy, shocked at the transformation in her dad, looked at the ground in embarrassment and started to walk towards the car. Jimmy stepped in front of her, and she stopped.

"Please calm down, Mr McDermott. I'm sorry we've deceived you, but you're getting angry over nothing. I love your daughter, and I think we should talk about this in private where we can be calm and sensible about it all. What do you think?"

It was the first time Jimmy said he loved her. Judy realised in that instant that she loved him too, but she also loved her dad. She was ashamed that she had lied to her parents.

Judy touched Jimmy's arm.

"It's OK, Jimmy," she said. "I'm going home with Dad. I'll get in touch with you tomorrow or the next day."

Judy slipped past Jimmy and got into the car. She studied her hands in her lap and didn't look up. She could hardly bear the humiliation.

"Right, you, whatever your name is," Jack McDermott growled at Jimmy, his index finger pointing up at his face. Jack realised that the young man was bigger than he was and looked like he could handle himself, but his rage held firm, and he wasn't afraid of what the young man could do. He was furious that he had some kind of hold over his daughter—his only child.

Jimmy held up a hand to try once again to placate the aggressor and perhaps calm down the volatile situation.

"My name is Jimmy, Jimmy Tucker, Mr McDermott, and I love your daughter."

Jimmy ignored the crowd surrounding them; he would face their jokes and leg-pulling later, when it had all calmed down, but at that moment, he felt he would say just about anything if it meant Judy's dad would at least understand how he felt about his daughter and allow them to continue seeing each other.

Jack McDermott stepped forward, his hands clenched in fists, his jaw jutting forward in an aggressive stance, like he had lost his mind and was about to start throwing punches.

The bikers saw the threat and began to react with the same level of aggression. Suddenly, it seemed as though a light went on in Jack McDermott's mind, and he saw the danger he'd put himself in. He blinked, and his fists unclenched. He shook his head like he'd come to his senses and took a step backward.

"Right then, Jimmy Tucker. Understand this carefully," he said with real conviction.

"Just you stay away from my daughter, you hear?"

He turned towards the car, but his path was blocked by the bikers. Judy saw her dad surrounded by the bikers she'd just started to get to know. Suddenly, she was afraid for her dad. She knew what they could do in a fair fight, and she was terrified that her dad would come to serious harm. She opened the car door and stood on the doorframe, holding on to the door for balance.

"Jimmy?" she shouted. "Is my dad ok? Don't hurt him. He's angry, but he loves me."

Jimmy craned his neck to see Judy. She was hidden by the crowd gathered around her dad.

"Let him through, guys," called Jimmy. He turned to Judy's dad.

"I'm sorry, Mr McDermott. I'll call round once the dust has settled."

The bikers parted and allowed him to pass. Jack McDermott took his chance and made for his car.

As they drove out of the bike park, Judy noticed Jokerman pulling in with Gerry on the back. She hoped that, in his fury, her dad had not noticed them. She didn't want this kind of trouble landing on Gerry if her dad told Gerry's dad what they'd been getting up to. Her dad was angry in a different way than he had been when he was confronting Jimmy, having suffered humiliation because his own teenage daughter had to stand up for him. He got into the car and drove back to Letchmore Heath in a furious silence, ignoring Judy's tears and apologies.

"I'm sorry I let you and Mum down. I was going to tell you all about him when the time was right, I promise," she said when they got home.

"Just leave it, Judy. I'm ashamed of you," came her dad's reply.

Judy's silent tears erupted into uncontrollable sobs at his words. When they arrived home, she fled to the door. The front door was locked, and she had to stand and wait until her mum unlocked it. Judy ran past her without a word, leaving her mum to stand bewildered, watching Judy run up the stairs and into her bedroom.

"Mary, she's not to go out again until I can trust her," said Jack as he stormed past his wife.

"What's going on, Jack?" replied Mary, following her husband into the hallway.

"You can't tell her she can't go out. She's almost an adult—she goes to college, for goodness' sake!"

Judy heard her mum's raised voice from her bedroom but couldn't hear what she had said and assumed she was as angry as her dad was. She buried her head in her pillow and wanted it all to go back to the way it had been that morning.

Mary went into the living room to question her husband.

"Jack, would you please tell me what's wrong? What on earth has happened?"

"She's been lying to us," he replied, pointing up in the direction of Judy's bedroom.

"Lies and more bloody lies! For weeks! No doubt about that. She's been gallivanting about on the back of a motorbike with no crash helmet on. God only knows what else she's been up to," yelled Jack.

"Judy! Get yourself down here, right now! We have things to talk about, my girl."

When Jack became angry and shouted, his Irish accent rose to the fore. The angrier he was, the more pronounced his accent became.

Judy could hardly decipher his words as he yelled at her to come down the stairs, but she knew just how much trouble she was in at that moment. Judy made her way reluctantly down the stairs. She stood in the doorway, listening to her dad's rage.

"A motorbike?" said Judy's mum, her hands held to her mouth. Judy went to her mum and wrapped her arms around her waist, like she had done when she was a small child.

"Oh Mum, I'm so sorry I didn't tell you about Jimmy," she said and broke down in floods of tears.

Her mum wrapped her arms around Judy's shoulders and cuddled her.

"Oh, love, why didn't you talk to us? Why lie? We would have listened."

"I just want to go to my room," sobbed Judy.

"Not so fast, my girl, not until we've talked about all of this," Jack McDermott snapped at his beleaguered daughter.

"Leave it, Jack. That's enough for tonight. Tomorrow she can stay home, and we can try to understand what this is all about," responded Mary. "Now off you go to bed, love, and don't worry too much. We can speak tomorrow."

Judy ran up the stairs and slammed the door of her bedroom in frustration and anger. She wiped her nose on a tissue, then fell face-down on the bed. Her tears made her mascara run, and she didn't really care whether her pillow was streaked with black. She sobbed until she fell asleep.

The Bombshell

Thursday 17th October 1963

Leaning forward in her seat so she could peer through the window, Gerry sat on the top deck of the number 311 bus to Watford as it passed Round Bush without stopping. She leaned back in her seat and feared the worst. She had seen Mr McDermott drive out of the Busy Bee with Judy crying in the seat beside him, and she knew what kind of ear-bashing Judy would have endured. His attention was focused on the road ahead; Gerry tried to convince herself that he had not seen her arrive on the back of Jokerman's bike. 'Poor Judy', she thought, 'and poor me if he's seen me and has plans to tell my dad.' Gerry didn't relish the thought of what would happen if Mr McDermott had seen her. She shivered at the consequences she might face. Jack McDermott had a short temper, but he wasn't as volatile as her own dad. Not by a long stretch.

Judy woke late. She picked up her bedside clock and sighed.

 "9am? I've missed college, then," she muttered to herself. Her mum had let her sleep in.

Judy washed, cleaned herself up, changed clothes and made her way downstairs, where her mum was cooking scrambled eggs on toast for their breakfast.

"Hello, love, you look only a little better than you did last night. Are you feeling peaky?" she asked.

Judy closed her eyes for a moment; the smell of the eggs overwhelmed her senses. A feeling of nausea washed over her, and her stomach flipped.

"Oh, no," she said and turned. She ran back up the stairs and into the bathroom, making it to the toilet just in time. Judy threw up a little bile and water; there was nothing else in her stomach, as she'd not eaten anything since leaving the house the night before. Gasping, she retched two or three times more, but there was nothing left in her stomach.

"Bloody hell," she whispered. "I didn't think things could get any worse than last night."

She cleaned herself up, wiped down the toilet and flushed it again, then made her way back downstairs.

"Sorry, Mum. I'm not hungry. Can I just have a cup of tea and a piece of toast, please?"

"Of course you can, love. Come and sit down—your dad will be home soon for a chat. Is there anything you want to tell me before he gets here?"

Judy burst into tears.

"Oh, Mum, I'm sorry. I love you and Dad so much, but I love Jimmy very much as well."

"Of course you do, love. I understand. I was young once. Young love is special. Do you have a problem? I mean, other than what happened last night, of course."

"I don't know, Mum. I just feel so very sorry that I lied to you and Dad. But I fell for Jimmy the moment he came into Mr Stephens' shop on the first day I started college. He's been on my mind ever since. We've had great times together. I know this is the real thing. Won't you and Dad just meet with him, please?"

Judy went forward and took hold of her mum's hand, trying to plead with her. Mary McDermott looked at her daughter, and, for once, she really studied her. She took hold of Judy's other hand and held them out to make a wide circle of their arms. She looked her daughter up and down and frowned.

"Answer this question first. Have you just been upstairs to be sick?" Judy couldn't look her mother in the eye, and she looked at the floor. "Judy, answer me."

Her mother's voice was stern, commanding an answer. Judy tried to let go of her mum's hands, but Mary held tight.

"You were sick this morning, weren't you? Do you think you may be pregnant? Is there any reason why you might be pregnant? Tell me please, Judy, what have you been doing?"

"I really don't know, Mum. It was just one time. I didn't think you could get caught the first time. And... and we were careful. We used protection." Judy broke free from her mother's grasp and sat at the table. She put her head onto her hands and sobbed. "My period's late. I've never been late before. Mum, we were careful, I promise we were. Oh, what a mess. Help me, Mum, please. What am I going to do?"

Both turned to look toward the front door. They heard the car pull up and waited for Jack to put his key in the door. Judy's mind went at a mile a minute, trying to think straight.

'I can't be pregnant; this is all a ridiculous coincidence. It'll all be all right in a moment, I'm sure. It must be a nightmare. This doesn't happen to girls like me; I have so much to look forward to. What would I do with a baby?'

When Jack opened the door, he could see Mary sitting at the kitchen table. She stood up and approached her husband.

"Is she up yet?" he asked. "I, well... we need a good chat with that girl, Mary."

"She's in the kitchen. But I need a chat with you first, Jack," she said, leading him into the living room.

"There may be a bigger problem facing us than just a few lies or riding on a motorbike without a crash helmet."

"Bigger problem? What bigger problem could there possibly be?"

"Sit down in the lounge. I'll get you a cup of tea and fill you in."

Jack was originally from Ireland and met Mary just before the Second World War in 1938. He had joined the British Army in the Irish Guards, based at the Wellington Barracks in St James Palace. Jack was from a Catholic family in Dublin, but knowing that war against Hitler's Germany was a distinct possibility, he wanted to do his bit. He was a mechanic in the Irish Guards. He met Mary at a dance in Pimlico in 1938. They fell in love, and when war broke out in 1939, they decided to marry each other despite the dangers that they faced.

After the war, Jack was demobbed, and they rented a cottage in Letchmore Heath, Hertfordshire. He set up his lawnmower sales and repair shop in Round Bush and was very successful. Judy was born in 1947. There were complications with the birth which left Mary unable to have more children.

Mary returned to the lounge, handed Jack his favourite mug filled with his brew and sat next to him on the sofa. She paused for a moment, took a deep breath, and began to speak.

"OK, love, there's no easy way to say this, so I'll come right out with it. Judy could be pregnant,"

Mary said in her usual unflappable way. "We need to stay calm and think through what we will do if she is."

"Pregnant?" said Jack, and drew one hand down his face as though trying to wipe it all away. "Bloody Nora, what a mess."

"The first thing we'll need to do is to find out if she is pregnant. Then, we can make a plan," Mary went on calmly.

"Make a plan?" said Jack, spilling his tea. "I'll tell you what we'll do if she is. We'll send her to Ireland. She can live with Erin until she has the baby. It can be put up for adoption straight away. Nobody round here needs to know. Judy can come home next year when it's all done and dusted. We can ask the college to allow her to restart the course next September when she gets home. Kind of a sabbatical. Yes, we'll call it a sabbatical."

Jack sipped his tea as he warmed to the idea that was forming in his mind.

"As for that... what's his name? That Jimmy fella. He doesn't need to know. Once we know if she is pregnant or not, I'll take Judy to that café, the Busy Bee, next week, and she can finish with him for good."

Mary sat and listened to her husband plan out their daughter's future. She looked composed on the outside, but inside, in her mind and her heart, she raged against his simple, brutal plan for their only child. Mary stood up and moved away from the sofa. She stood with her back to her husband for a few moments.

She must have been thinking deeply, Jack assumed. Then she turned to face him, and his usually serene and collected wife stood before him in as much of a rage as he had seen her, since the first time he laid eyes on her at that dance in Pimlico, just before the war.

"Well, Jack McDermott, you seem to have it all worked out, don't you? What about me? I suppose I don't get a say in the matter. What about Judy? I think you've forgotten the problems I had when I was carrying Judy. I might remind you that she may just take after me in that respect. What happens if there are complications in her child's birth, like there were in ours? She might not get another chance to have another baby—just like me! And you want her to give all that up, just because you're worried about what the neighbours will think?" Mary's voice cracked, and she broke down in tears.

Jack sat on the sofa, open-mouthed. His Irish upbringing and army training shoved to the fore of his thought process, and he matched Mary's outrage and anger. He stood up. His favourite mug dropped to the floor and the handle broke off. He didn't notice.

"Enough, Mary! My mind is made up. It'll be best for everyone. Judy will get herself together and put her life back on track. We can save any embarrassment, not only for her but for us, too.

It will be better for the child if it goes to a loving, caring home." Jack announced. "My mind is made up."

He took a faltering step forward and made a half-hearted attempt to put his arm around his wife, but she shrugged off the effort.

"Not much point me talking to Judy now. Get the test sorted first, then we'll know what to do. Either way, she will finish with that boy. I'm off back to work."

Jack turned abruptly so Mary couldn't see the tears in his eyes.

From the kitchen table, Judy had heard everything her parents had said. She sat, her eyes filled with tears and her mouth agape. The harrowing details of the complications connected with her birth came as a shock to her; she had never realised the reason behind her being an only child. The full implications of what would happen if she were to suffer the same complications in the birth of her own child, meaning she would be unable to have any more, were not lost on her. If she had to give up her baby and she couldn't have any more, what use was she? In a world where women had few responsibilities beyond the household tasks of cleaning, cooking and childcare, if she couldn't have children, what would she do then?

Not many men would be willing to forego children because of a mistake his future wife made before they even met, and her dad had made it perfectly clear that Jimmy, the one who should share the responsibility, was to be cut out of her life without even knowing what she was going through. None of it seemed fair, and she could do nothing about it all, it seemed.

She ran upstairs to her room, heartbroken. She spent the rest of the day in her bed, dozing and thinking about her limited options, punctuated by bouts of crying. Her mum brought a supper tray at around 6. She ate most of the sausage, mash and greens but fell asleep early, emotionally exhausted.

Friday 18ᵗʰ October 1963

Judy woke early. At first, her thoughts consisted of the usual Friday tasks before college, and then reality slammed into her mind with the memories of the previous few days. She groaned like an old woman with decades of residual aches and pains to deal with. She sat up, swung her legs over the side of the bed and thought about what had happened, how fast it had all happened and what she could do to try and fix everything that was going wrong in her life.

"I hope this is some kind of nightmare," she said quietly. "I really do hope I will wake up from this because I'm already sick to death of all the drama. Can I just get back to being me?"

The reflection in her mirror told her the harsh truth. It was not a nightmare that she could wake up from. It was the other kind—a nightmare that she would have to live with forever. Her eyes were puffy, and her dark shadows looked like she'd gone overboard with the makeup and put the eyeshadow in entirely the wrong place. She was thankful that she hadn't applied her mascara at all yesterday, because it would clearly have been a waste of time and effort, not to mention mascara.

Another mortifying train of thought hit her heart, and she felt the weight of it sinking in her chest.

'Did he mean it? Would Dad really banish me to Ireland, to Aunt Erin's? Would he force me to give up my baby, return to Letchmore Heath and act as if nothing happened? Worst of all, would he insist that I tell Jimmy that we're through? That I can never see him again? I couldn't bear it.'

A form of grief overwhelmed her. Her eyes filled with tears, and she wiped her face with both hands in a feeble attempt to stop herself from crying. She thought she had gotten her emotions under control when nausea took over. She rushed to the bathroom and puked up the meal her mum had brought her the previous evening. She puked up bile, water, and, she believed, every hope and dream she ever had. The retching continued until there was nothing left in her stomach.

"Bloody hell," she muttered. "How has this happened? We were so careful."

She cleaned herself up, washed, got ready to go to college and then remembered she had an appointment at the Red House doctor's surgery in Radlett. Her mum would be with her.

She went downstairs. Her dad was standing in the kitchen.

"Dad, I'm so sorry. Please forgive me," she pleaded.

Jack McDermott looked at her with a stony expression.

"It's a bit late for all that now, young lady. Once we have the results of the test, we'll sit down and discuss your future. In the meantime, you're grounded. You'll help your mum around the house.

I'm off to work now, so do as you're told."

His expression remained stern, he pushed past his daughter and left for work.

"Hello, love, how do you feel this morning?" Judy's mum asked as she came down the stairs.

"I heard you being sick again this morning. It all looks quite bleak, I'm afraid. Our appointment with the doctor is at 10.30 this morning, so there's just enough time for some tea and toast."

"Mum, I heard what Dad said last night. If I am pregnant, I don't want to go to Ireland. I don't want to give up my baby. I don't want to finish with Jimmy," Judy pleaded. She broke down in tears again.

"Come on, love, let's not jump to conclusions. We should wait until we've seen the doctor this morning. Now, finish your tea and toast. It's a long walk to the Red House surgery, so we'd best get going."

When they arrived at the surgery, they checked in with the receptionist. "Good morning, Mary," said the portly lady behind the counter. "How can I help you?"

"Good morning, Phillis. We have an appointment with Dr Wodge at 10:30."

"Ah yes, you're all booked in for 10:30. He's running a little late, but I'll call you when he's ready for you," replied Phyllis. "How are you, love? I haven't seen you in ages. And this must be Judy! My, you have grown. The last time I saw you, you were just a nipper."

"Yes, it's been a while. We're all fine. How's your David? Is he still working at Sellotapes in Borehamwood? We must meet you for a drink sometime at the Cat and Fiddle."

"Yes, David is still at Sellotapes," replied Phillis, "although some new production line is being installed and there are rumours of redundancies to come, but we hope not yet."

Judy listened to their banal conversation for only a couple of sentences before zoning out. She didn't like the look on Phillis's face. She had a suspicious, knowing look about her. Judy could bet that she enjoyed working there because of the potential for gossip.

'Oh, Judy McDermott's pregnant, you know, and Mr Such-and-such from up the road has a bad case of the clap. His wife left him a few months ago—I wonder if that was the reason? Mrs So-and-so is drinking again... yes, I know... Mother's Ruin, they used to call it.' Judy's thoughts were probably close to the truth.

The waiting room had reams of information in leaflet form scattered on the coffee table. Anything from piles to arthritis. Then, Judy noticed one that was simply titled 'Pregnant'. She shuffled in her chair nervously.

At 10.35, the buzzer sounded. A light flashed against Dr Wodge's name on the wall. He was in surgery number two today. They got up, made their way to surgery number two and knocked on the door.

"Come in," boomed the friendly voice of Dr Wodge.

He was not the most senior doctor at the surgery but had been there for over 5 years. Mary knew him well. He had a very kindly manner and always seemed to care and listen carefully to whatever concerns people had.

"Good morning, Doctor," said Mary. "How are you and the family?"

"All good, thanks, Mary. Take a seat, both of you."

Turning to look at Judy, he said, "And you must be Judy. I haven't seen you since your BCG vaccination some four years ago, as it says here on your records."

He looked over his half-rimmed reading glasses with a warm, caring expression. "How can I help?" he said, looking at Judy.

"Well, Doctor, the thing is..." Mary started to reply.

"I asked Judy, thank you, Mary," the doctor interrupted.

Judy had once again zoned out and was staring at the floor. She glanced up with tears in her eyes. She looked at Doctor Wodge. She felt that she could confide in the kindly-looking man. She tried to speak, but her mouth was dry, and she struggled to get any words out.

"I er, I er, I think..." she stammered. "I might be pregnant, Doctor." Judy surprised herself when she finally found the strength to say what had been running through her mind since the morning after her dad had dragged her from the Busy Bee.

"And what makes you think that, Judy?" he asked.

Mary leaned forward, placing one hand on the desk between herself and the doctor.

"She has been..." she started to say, but the doctor held up his hand and gave her a discouraging glance. Then his attention went back to focus on Judy, and his expression became kind again.

"I asked Judy, Mary. I'm afraid that I must ask you to allow her to speak for herself."

"My period is over two weeks late, and I'm never late. I've been very sick the last couple of mornings. I can't face breakfast without throwing up," Judy said in a quiet, miserable voice.

"Have you any other reasons to think you might be pregnant? For example, have you had any physical relationships recently? Judy, have you participated in sexual intercourse?" Dr Wodge studied her with a friendly expression. Judy felt less uncomfortable and eventually decided that she could speak freely to him, even in front of her mum.

"Yes, Doctor, but we were very careful. We used protection. It was my first time. He said that it was his first time as well. I didn't think you could get pregnant the first time."

She put her hands over her face and started to sob.

"There, there, Judy. Let's get this all sorted out. I would like a sample of your urine, please," he said. He wrote her name and date of birth on a sticky label and applied it to a screw-top glass bottle. "Do you think you could manage that for me, please?"

Judy nodded, picked up the bottle, left the surgery and made for the toilet.

Whilst she was gone, Doctor Wodge explained to Mary that it was important that Judy spoke and took responsibility for whatever condition she was in for herself. He told Mary that from everything Judy has described, it would seem highly likely that she was pregnant, but a test would provide confirmation.

Judy returned with the sample bottle filled as full as she could manage. Doctor Wodge thanked her and explained that the result would take up to two weeks to come through.

Dr Wodge peered over the top of his half-rimmed glasses, and with a friendly smile, he noted, "Judy, I think from the symptoms you have described and the fact that your period is late despite being on time since they started, it is highly likely that you are pregnant. Until we get the test result, we cannot be sure for certain. As soon as we have the result, I will let you know. In the meantime, try to relax and think about your future."

They left the surgery and walked back to Letchmore Heath. The sun was shining, and although the leaves had still not turned, they could feel an autumn chill in the air. Judy thought to herself that she had not lived yet; was she going into the autumn of her life already?

As they made their way down Common Lane to Letchmore Heath, Judy vowed to herself that she would remain strong. Even if the pregnancy test result confirmed that she was pregnant, she would make something of her life, no matter what was thrown at her.

When Jack returned home that evening, Mary described what Dr Wodge had said and that the test result would be back in around two weeks.

"So let me get this straight," said Jack, "the doctor thinks it highly likely that she is pregnant, but the test will confirm it or not in two weeks?"

"Yes, that's right, love," replied Mary. Hoping that Jack would not take any rash decisions until the test result was back, she went on, "I think we should carry on as normal until we have confirmation of the situation."

"Not on your nelly," Jack responded with a raised voice, "we can't wait that long. I've heard enough. Get Judy in here now.
Mary called Judy to the sitting room.

"Sit down, Judy. We have a great deal to talk about," he said in a less kindly manner than Doctor Wodge had used.

Mary came in with the tea. Jack started his well-rehearsed rant. "Now, you listen to me, my girl, you've let me and your mum down. But most importantly, you've let yourself down when you have—or rather, you had—your whole life ahead of you. And what for? Some grubby moment with, what's his name, er, er, Jimmy?"

"It wasn't like that, Dad," Judy sobbed. "I love him, and besides, we still need to confirm that I am pregnant."

"I've heard enough to know that you are pregnant, and as for love?" Jack snorted derision at her protestation.

"What do you think that is, eh? I'll tell you what love should be. It should be showing respect for what your mother and I have done for you; we've cared and looked after you for seventeen years.

And this is the way you repay us. With a grubby one-night stand?

Well, let me tell you how we're going to deal with this sordid situation." Red in the face, Jack's anger knew no bounds. He went on,

"I've been in touch with your Aunt Erin in Dublin. She's agreed that you can live there until this baby is born. Nobody knows you there, so there won't be any embarrassment. Once the baby's born, it can go up for adoption. You can come home next June. You'll have to start your course again in September next year, but at least you can get your life back on track and put this silly episode behind you."

"But Dad, I don't want to go to Dublin. I don't want to give up this baby if I am pregnant. I want to stay here and work it out with Jimmy." Judy raised her voice to match his and was almost screaming at him.

"What you want is of no consequence, young lady. I've made up my mind. Your mum and I will drive you to Holyhead, and we'll catch the ferry to Dublin next weekend. Tickets have been arranged. We'll stay with you for a day or so, then we'll come home. Erin has a telephone, so I can call from the workshop once a week to check how you're doing."

Jack paced the room, thinking. Judy and Mary sat in silence as they waited for him to deliver more of his rules and declarations for what was in store for Judy and her child.

"On Wednesday, I'll take you to the Busy Bee. You can finish with this Jimmy fella once and for all so that he doesn't bother us whilst you're gone.

You won't tell him what's happened, only that you're going away and don't want to see him anymore. Understood?"

He waited for it all to sink in, but when Judy stared blankly at him without agreeing to his demands, he snapped at her, making her jump.

"Answer me! Is that understood?"

Judy was numb with fear at the prospect of going away just to save them all from the embarrassment of her pregnancy. The prospect of returning without her baby as if nothing had ever happened terrified her. She was beyond crying; she had no anger left in her, just an empty, desolate feeling of submission and despair. All her ambitions for life had disintegrated in just a few weeks.

She nodded submissively, then left the room and went upstairs, completely lost in total shock at the brutality of the plan her dad outlined.

Monday 21ˢᵗ October 1963

The weekend was a quiet one. Mary McDermott let the Bishop's supermarket manager know that Judy was unwell and would not be at work. Judy yearned to speak to Gerry, but it was impossible. She was grounded. The only phone she had access to was in the telephone box by the green. Gerry did not have a telephone at her house, so there was no way she could contact Gerry other than by sending a letter, and she did not want to risk anything in writing that could be intercepted by Gerry's parents.

Jimmy tried to contact Judy. He knocked on the door on Saturday morning. There was no answer.

He pushed a note through the letterbox. Jack McDermott found it and promptly tore it to pieces.

Judy woke up early on Monday morning. After the usual ritual of throwing up, she got ready and prepared herself for a week at home before being banished to Ireland even before it was officially confirmed that she was indeed pregnant. But she knew deep down that she was pregnant. The test result was just a formality. The morning sickness had continued so relentlessly that she had almost gotten used to the vomiting.

"Dad, you're still here. No work today?" asked Judy as she entered the kitchen.

"No, I'll open the shop a little later this morning. I've stayed back just to make sure that you know that you are grounded until we head off to Ireland this weekend."

"Dad, I don't want to…" she started to explain.

Jack lifted his hand and turned his face away from her to show that he wasn't listening.

"Not now, Judy, or later. It's not just about what you want."

His mind was made up.

He kissed his wife and left to go to his workshop, satisfied that he had put his foot down and that everyone knew where they stood. At the very least, he had avoided any embarrassment and provided a plan that would enable Judy to recover her life and start again.

Or so he thought.

Judy looked at her mum with tears streaming down her cheeks. "He's not going to listen, is he, Mum?"

"Come on, love. Finish your tea and toast. Then we can set about packing and preparing for your trip. Once your dad has made up his mind, it is very difficult to get him to consider anything else, I'm afraid, love."

Judy was almost frozen with fear at the fate that awaited her in Ireland. But first, she had to face Jimmy and tell him that they were through. Her heart sank at the thought; she descended into a dark depression and switched into automatic mode to see out the week.

Breaking Up

Wednesday 23rd October 1963

Judy had spent the last couple of days packing and coming to terms with her fate. Her mother informed the manager at Bishop's supermarket that Judy would not be returning to work. Her dad spoke to someone at Casio College and arranged for Judy to take a year's sabbatical. She would restart her course in September 1964.

She knew she had no choice in the matter. She tried to prepare herself for seeing Jimmy that evening, dreading his reaction.

The Busy Bee was buzzing with excitement; it was record night. Although the weather was poor, drizzling and threatening rain, everyone looked forward to a fun time. Everyone, that is, except Jimmy. He was subdued, bordering on depression, and had not been himself since Judy left the car park with her dad a week ago. It was difficult not to notice his glum expression.

The lads were careful not to make jokes about girls or girlfriends because they could see that one of their best friends was hurting badly.

The jukebox played 'Let There Be Drums' by Sandy Nelson, the pinball machines were in full use, the air was thick with cigarette smoke and the window front was steamed up, preventing a clear view of the bikes parked outside. Gerry and Jokerman sat at the back of the café, concerned about Jimmy and wondering what on earth had happened to Judy.

"Have you been round to her house to find out what's been happening?" Jokerman asked.

"No, I was waiting to see if she got in touch with me first," Gerry said. "I suppose I should have made the effort, but I feel awkward about trying to contact her now. It's a bit late for it now, isn't it?"

Gerry felt bad about not contacting her best friend. She knew her own dad would have grounded her if the situation had been reversed, but Gerry didn't want to risk confrontation if Judy's dad answered the door. Gerry sat and nursed her drink; she missed Judy, and college wasn't the same without her. She couldn't seem to concentrate.

Nobody noticed Jack's Morris Minor pull into the car park. Judy opened the car door, but Jack placed his hand firmly on her arm and held her back.

"OK, you call him outside and tell him straight that you're through and that you're going away. Tell him that you won't be seeing him again. Tell him that, and nothing else. Have you got that, my girl?" Jack growled.

Judy nodded and got out of the car. She went towards the café. As she got to it, the door flew open and Turd rushed past her.

He ran across to mount his bike and get to the Elstree Res roundabout to check on the record night riders as he always did on record night. He stumbled momentarily when he saw Judy but thought better of it. He kept going, jumped onto his Indian Scout, kick-started the bike, and rode out onto the A41.

The door stood open. Everyone could see Judy standing just outside. The noise in the café dropped, and it went very quiet. Jimmy looked up and saw Judy at the doorway. She looked sad, bedraggled and completely lost. He jumped up from the bar. He ran across the room to her, and the crowd parted to let him through. She put up her hand, warning him not to embrace her, and took a step backwards, so they both ended up outside.

She looked up at him with tears in her eyes. He went to hold her, and she backed off.

"No, Jimmy, I can't. Please understand that I can't."

He put a finger to his lips and made a shushing noise. He took a ring from his finger and gave it to her. She took it without looking at it, dropping it into her pocket.

"Jimmy, I don't expect you to understand," she said, fighting back the tears. "But I can't see you again. I'm going away. We're through." She broke down in floods of tears. "Please forgive me, Jimmy, and please leave my parents alone while I'm away. I must go. Bye, Jimmy."

With that, she turned and made her way back to her dad's car. She felt wretched about how she'd left him like that. Standing in front of the Busy Bee café, for all the world to see his humiliation and desperation.

"Wait!" Jimmy called after her. He watched her as she walked towards a car, the same car she had been forced into just a week ago. "What have I done? Why is this happening?"

Judy got into her dad's car, but she stopped momentarily from closing the door and therefore briefly stopped him from taking her away, back home, back to the misery of her new future.

She watched as Jimmy ran inside the café. He grabbed his crash helmet, which he seldom wore, put a record on the jukebox and ran to his bike. He was crying, tears running down his face, and he didn't want anyone to see those tears. The record he put on was 'Leader of the Pack' by the Shangri-Las.

He kick-started his bike.

"Judy, close that bloody door now!" Jack demanded.

She closed the door reluctantly, and Jack began to move the car out of the car park.

Jimmy, on his bike, shot from the car park, almost colliding with Jack McDermott's car as he accelerated away up the A41.

Judy gasped in horror as she watched Jimmy tear away recklessly up the road.

"Please, Dad, can't we wait here to see that he gets back safely?"

"No, Judy, it's done. We must all move on."

Jack was determined. There was no point in arguing anymore.

Jimmy could hardly see for the tears streaming down his face. His vision blurred by his tears, and the drizzle which had turned into rain impeded his vision to almost non-existence. His riding was almost out of control. He rounded the roundabout at breakneck speed. Turd was confused to see Jimmy first up on record night and quickly realised that something was seriously wrong. After a moment's thought, he realised something must have happened between Jimmy and Judy. A look of deep concern came upon Turd's face. He knew that emotions, motorbikes, speed and wet weather were a cocktail for disaster.

Jimmy accelerated hard along the treacherous road. The rain was falling heavily by now. The café emptied. Everyone realised that Jimmy had gone on the record run without telling anyone. They stood out in the rain and watched the entire length of the A41, concerned for the safety of one of their own.

Jimmy overtook everything he encountered on the road. He made no judgement call about whether the road was clear or even if it was safe to overtake. Faster and faster, he pushed his machine on beyond his capabilities, beyond the endurance of the bike beneath him. Suddenly, without warning, his bike snaked. He lost control. The front wheel hit something—probably the kerb—and stopped the bike dead in its tracks. Jimmy was thrown into the air, narrowly missing an oncoming car.

His bike cartwheeled alongside him. He bounced on to the grass verge, just missing a tree, breaking an arm and his right leg in the fall. His bike crashed to a standstill just yards from him. The petrol tank burst into flames.

In the dark, wet and miserable night, visibility was low, but Jokerman saw the flames in the distance and just knew it was something to do with Jimmy. Jokerman jumped on his bike, kick-started it and rushed away to help his friend. Everyone at the Busy Bee stood by, fearing the worse.

"Call an ambulance!" Jokerman yelled at the crowd as he exited the bike park. Roaring up the road towards the roundabout, towards the scene of the accident, where Jimmy lay unconscious.

Jokerman closed in on the scene of the crash and braked hard, skidding to a halt. He dropped his bike before he'd even had time to stop, not worried about his own safety or that of his bike, and he ran towards the site of the explosion. He saw a body lying on the ground close to the burning bike. It was Jimmy. He could see that his arm was broken by the way Jimmy held it, trying to protect it from more damage and trying to minimise the pain. He grabbed Jimmy by his other arm and pulled, dragging Jimmy away from the burning wreckage. Fearing that Jimmy's bike might blow up any minute, he didn't stop dragging until Jimmy suddenly yelled at him.

"Bloody leave me alone, will you? You're doing more damage to my leg!"

Jimmy lapsed back into unconsciousness, and Jokerman turned him on to his back, trying to find signs of life.

"Come on, mate, hang in there," he muttered. "Don't leave me. An ambulance is on its way." He thought he saw Jimmy's eyelids flicker. He added, "That's good, mate; we'll get you out of here. Just stay with it."

Jokerman could hear a bell in the distance; it was the sound of the ambulance coming at full speed. He cradled his friend's head in his arms until the ambulance arrived. They quickly attended to Jimmy.

"Don't worry too much, lad," the attending ambulance driver said. "It looks like he's still alive."

The police arrived and wanted statements from everyone. Jimmy was taken to Watford Hospital.

The record finished on the jukebox: The leader of the pack, and now he's gone, the leader of the pack, and now he's gone. But Jimmy had not gone. He had survived. His crash helmet had saved him. After two months in Watford hospital, he was home to convalesce with his mum looking after him. Judy was never far from his thoughts. He was confused. He needed answers. Why had she left? Where had she gone? People don't just disappear. He vowed that once he was fully recovered, he would get the answers he needed.

Nightmare in Ireland

Saturday 26th October 1963

Jack loaded up the car, and they left at 5am for the drive to Holyhead, North Wales. It was a very long journey. Judy slept most of the way, waking only when they stopped for a cup of tea and a toilet break. They arrived late in the afternoon. The sailing was a night crossing. The ferry was fully loaded by 3am on the Sunday morning.

The sea was rough, with a high wind violently rocking the ferry. Many people suffered from seasickness caused by the stormy seas. Being sick was second nature to Judy by now, so she was not as troubled by it as her mum and dad were. Both hated the journey and were sick most of the way.

Judy couldn't stop thinking about Jimmy. Was he OK? Did he have a crash on that awful night? She vowed that she would return one day to uncover the answers she needed.

Sunday 27th October 1963

Once they had docked and the ferry had unloaded, they drove through customs and past the train station. They stopped at a café for tea and an early breakfast before setting off for Beaver Close in Dublin, where Erin, Judy's aunt, lived with her husband, Patrick. They arrived at 10.30am and parked and unloaded the car. Erin, Jack's youngest sister, was in her early thirties with red hair, a buxom figure and a cheeky smile.

"Hello, love," she said to her brother, giving him a big hug. "And look at you, Mary. You haven't changed a bit since I last saw you. What is it? Nine or ten years since we were last together?"

Turning to Judy, she placed her hands on her hips and appraised her young niece. "You must be Judy. You were around eight when I last saw you. My, you have grown. Got some growing to do now, too, no doubt."

She grinned and wagged her finger at Judy.

"Come on in, all of you. Let me introduce you to Patrick, my husband these past six years. Such a shame that you couldn't come over for the wedding," she said through gritted teeth.

"Top o' the morning to you all!" Patrick boomed a greeting with a glint in his eye and a wink at the lasses as he stood up to meet them. Patrick was a big man, around six feet four inches tall. He too had red hair and a fair complexion, with freckles and a beer gut to behold. He gave them all a hug, holding onto Judy a little longer than he should have and a little tighter than was comfortable for her.

"Well, Jack, you've arrived in time for the pub to open, so let's get your bags unloaded, and we can be at the pub for noon. We'll be back by three, Erin, love, just in time for dinner," he said. He ushered Jack out of the door. The two men unloaded the bags and headed to the pub.

Right after Sunday dinner, Judy thought all the adults had dozed off on the sofa or had gone to bed for a nap. She was in the kitchen, cleaning away the plates. She realised that someone had approached and was standing in the doorway, watching her.

"Hello, Uncle Patrick," she said. "I thought you would have gone for a sleep."

He was still swaying a little from his session at the pub and the additional beers he'd put away at dinner.

"You're a pretty young thing," he whispered to Judy as he staggered forward towards her. "I'm looking forward to having you around. Maybe we can get better acquainted when Erin is at work. What do you think?"

Judy was a little scared. She scanned the draining board for a knife, just in case.

"I don't think that would be appropriate, Uncle Patrick. Now, why not sit down with the others while I finish clearing up?"

Patrick snarled. He shrugged his shoulders and staggered back to the sitting room.

Monday 28th October 1963

After breakfast, Jack loaded up the car and got ready to leave to catch the midday ferry crossing.

Mary hugged her daughter and whispered in her ear, "Be brave, my darling girl. This is all for the best in the long run."

She had to turn away quickly to hide the fact that she was crying.

Judy held on to her mother, her tears flowing freely.

"Please, Mum, let me come back with you. I don't want to stay here. I don't want to give up my baby."

"Come on, you two! That's enough tears. We must get moving. This is best for everyone, and we have to leave right now to get the ferry," said Jack firmly.

With that, he ushered his wife toward the car. He shook Patrick's hand and hugged his sister. Thanking them for their help, Jack reconfirmed that he would send them money every month as a thank you for caring for his daughter. With that, he attempted to hug Judy. She took a step back and shook her head. She refused to look him in the eye, instead looking down at the ground.

"Oh well, young lady, you'll thank me for doing this, one day," Jack said. He jumped in the car and drove away without looking back.

"Right, that's over with," Erin spoke in a tone which made Judy feel uneasy. "Inside, you. I need to go over a few rules whilst you're staying here."

Erin pushed Judy into the house.

Inside the house, Erin pushed Judy towards the kitchen. She backed her up until her legs came up against a chair, and Erin pushed her further back until she sat down. "Right, now you listen to me, you feckin' little whore," she snarled. "Whilst you're here, you stay away from my Patrick. You keep on top of the housework, cleaning, laundry and cooking, got it?"

Judy nodded, fear etched on her face.

Erin was becoming agitated. "My Patrick is like any other man. Having a pretty young thing in the house is one thing, but a young, pretty whore might give him ideas. If I catch you egging him on, or not keeping up with your feckin' work, I'll march you to the Magdalene Laundry on Killarney Street, where you'll remain until you've had this baby. After that, you can feck off back to England. You got that?"

Judy sat on the chair, not daring to move. She was stunned, but she found herself nodding nervously. What was the Magdalene Laundry on Killarney Street? She had no idea. She assumed it was a worse nightmare than the one she found herself in now. She stopped nodding. She found some courage to speak.

"Why did you agree to have me here? You clearly don't want me here, do you?"

"Simple, love. It's the money. That's why you're here. Don't think I won't send you to the Magdalene Laundry. I'll still make money doing it that way as well. Don't even think about bleating to my brother, either, because he might be your da, but he will believe me over you, given what you've been up to as of late." As she finished speaking, she laughed. Erin grabbed her stomach and wobbled it up and down.

"Now, you can start by stripping our bed, doing the washing and hoovering the house. Monday is washing day, after all." She laughed again, louder than before.

Judy fell into a dark mental state almost as soon as her parents left her with her aunt. How did she go from having her whole life ahead of her, having fun and endless prospects, to this wretched state? For one moment, she thought about running away. Then she thought better about that idea. Where would she go? She had no money, Erin held her passport, she was alone in Ireland, and she didn't know anybody. The feelings of despair deepened. Then she thought that the only thing she could do was to get on with it and do as she was told. She fell into a deep depression.

A week later, Erin grinned at Judy.

"Your Da called yesterday to say that the doctor had confirmed that you are pregnant, but I guess you knew that anyway."

This news was no surprise to Judy. She guessed that her parents were satisfied that they had not waited for the result before condemning her to this hellhole.

Friday 22nd November 1963

Almost four weeks since her parents left to go back to England, Judy was working harder than at any time in her life. Erin rigorously inspected every task Judy was set. If she was not satisfied, she would undo the work and make Judy start all over again. Erin sat with her feet up most days, listening to the wireless, eating toffees and chain-smoking cigarettes. She would call from the living room and demand a cup of tea. Even if Judy was upstairs, cleaning the bedrooms, or outside, sweeping the yard, she would have to break off and make Erin that cup of tea.

"You took your feckin' time about it," she snarled this time.

"I was at the bottom of the yard, moving the dustbins," protested Judy. "I don't think I should be moving heavy dustbins, Aunt Erin. What about the baby?"

"The baby! Do you mean that bastard you're carrying? So what if you lost it by hefting those bins around? That would be a blessing. I'd be doing you a favour!"

Judy's eyes pricked with tears at her callous words. She turned away from her aunt because she didn't want to give her the satisfaction of seeing her upset. That was the first time Judy's kind heart turned a little cold. She even contemplated spitting in the teapot before serving her aunt the tea.

Judy jumped out of her skin when Erin crept up behind her and spoke next to her ear.

"Don't you go thinking any nasty thoughts, you horrible little slut," she said. "Don't you be putting anything in my tea."

When Judy realised her thoughts and new-found nastiness were aligned with her aunt's, she decided that she would never stoop to her level again; she would never sink so low.

"I wouldn't do anything like that, Aunt Erin," she said. "I'm not that type of slut."

That one spark of rebelliousness shone in her eye as she spoke, and Erin saw it. Before Judy knew what had happened, Erin lashed out a hand to slap her around the face. Judy reeled at the sting. Erin was well-practised in the art of the face slap; she used minimum effort for maximum effect. The tears Judy had successfully hidden from her aunt before sprang to her eyes again and ran down her face.

"Get me that cup of tea and then get out of my sight," growled Erin. She didn't need to raise her voice or threaten to hit her again, as Judy knew where she stood, and she also knew there was no way out of the situation.

Judy could handle the days, but as soon as Patrick came home from working at the Guinness Brewery, she retired to her room to spend as much time there as she could. Patrick grew bolder in his lecherous comments and creepy offers to 'make her feel better'. There had been four or five occasions recently where Patrick stopped in the hallway, blocking her path, a leery grin on his face, his mottled tongue licking his lips, suggesting they 'have a cuddle when Erin goes out'. The first two times he offered, Judy stood transfixed, mortified at his brazenness. The last few times, she saw it for what it was: a power play, something to give him a buzz because he knew she couldn't do anything about his advances—neither telling her aunt nor her parents—because no one would believe her. They would think she was making up lies to get out of her situation.

Judy stayed out of Patrick's way as much as possible but sensed Erin's jealousy. Erin noticed and was becoming concerned at the attention Patrick showed Judy. She grew angry with each comment from him, acting as though it was her fault. Erin cornered Judy just after catching Patrick trying to 'smell Judy's perfume'.

"I'm not wearing perfume, Uncle Patrick," she said and tried to duck and back away. Patrick saw his wife watching from a doorway and turned and went back the way he'd just come.

"I see what you're doing, you little slut. Keep your hands off my husband," she grunted.

"But Aunt Erin…" Judy began to protest. Her words trailed off and she stopped speaking. It would do no good—Erin wouldn't believe she wasn't enticing Patrick.

Erin pointed her finger in Judy's face. Judy had nowhere to go, and her head bumped the wall behind her.

"I'll be taking you to the Magdalene Laundry if it carries on; you mark my words."

Judy tried to lean away from that pointing finger.

"It's not my fault…" she protested.

Erin replied, "Once a slut, always a slut."

However, that day, after tea at just after 7pm, the wireless news carried a shock announcement: President John F. Kennedy had been shot in the head during an open-top motorcade in Dallas, Texas. He had been rushed to hospital but was not expected to live. Erin almost collapsed in a heap at the news. She was a practising Catholic. With JFK being the first Catholic president, the news threw Erin into grief that Judy had not witnessed before, even at home. Erin fell to her knees. She knelt on the threadbare carpet in front of the fireplace, holding her rosary beads, repeating the 'Hail Mary' prayer over and over again.

Then the wireless announced the dreadful news that JFK was dead, despite the best efforts of the surgeons. "*Tonight, the world is in shock.*

John F. Kennedy, the 35th President of the United States of America, has been assassinated. He was only 43 years old," crackled the wireless. Erin let out a dramatic cry at the news. She renewed her sobbing, and she continued to pray. Patrick stood up, grabbed his coat and shook his head at his wife's back.

"I'm off to the pub," he said. "I need to get out of this house full of wailing women. I'll get more sense from the fellers at the pub."

Judy didn't know what to do or to say. Erin continued to rock back and forth on her knees, deep in prayer. She thought the best thing to do was ensure the kitchen work was finished, then make herself scarce by going to her room. At around 10pm, she heard a commotion outside as Patrick fell over the dustbins she had put out earlier. Patrick came home steaming drunk.

"Well, woman, what do you think of that?" he slurred, shoving open the kitchen door. "The world has gone feckin' mad when the president of the United States of America is shot in broad daylight!"

"You're swaying; look at you," Erin replied bitterly. "These days, you're either working, leering at young girls or drunk. The most powerful man in the world, a Catholic at that, gets shot, and what do you do? You take yourself off to the pub and get drunk, you useless man!"

"Don't you talk to me like that, you fat cow!"

Patrick yelled at her.

He raised his hand and slapped Erin across her face, knocking her to the floor. Judy crept to the top of the stairs to listen.

"I'm off to bed now. When I wake up, I want you to have made plans for that girl to leave. She can have her baby somewhere else so we can get back to normal," Patrick hollered and stormed off.

Judy was quick to dash back into her room, close the door and pretend to be asleep. She heard Patrick collapse into his bed in the next room. Erin made her way upstairs sobbing. Judy wasn't sure if she was crying because of President Kennedy's death or because Patrick had slapped her about. She was sure that she was in a dangerous place. Perhaps somewhere else really was a better place to be.

Monday 25th November 1963

The weekend had been tense. Patrick went to the pub on Saturday and Sunday, returning drunk both nights. Erin, nursing a black eye, kept out of his way, whilst Judy kept busy with the chores.

When Judy woke on Monday morning, she heard Patrick and Erin arguing again. She couldn't hear clearly, but she got the gist of the argument. It was about her. Erin accused Patrick of flirting with her. Patrick denied it, accusing Judy of giving him the come-on. Judy was shocked. She had tried to keep her nose clean and stay out of the way as much as she could. Then Erin raised her voice even louder.

"That's it! I've had enough. I'm putting that whore into the Magdalene Laundry on Killarney Street today. She can stay there until her bastard is born, then adopted, and she can go back to England."

Judy listened as the people she counted on for her care in this almost foreign country screamed at each other. She caught sight of her reflection in the mirror in her bedroom.

'What a bloody mess!' she thought. Then she shook her head and mouthed, 'No! What a fucking mess. A fucking, fucking mess.'

She got dressed and braced herself for what she already knew was going to happen. When she arrived at the kitchen, Erin had changed her tone. "Judy love, your uncle Patrick and I have had a chat. We've made the decision that it would be best for everyone if you spent the rest of the time until the baby is born at the Magdalene Laundry.

The nuns that run the place are familiar with the challenges young girls face when dealing with unplanned pregnancies. I spoke to the Mother Superior last week about your situation. Bless her, she's agreed to accept you into the institution. It's a place where you'll live and work with other girls that are pregnant."

"But..." Judy started to protest.

Erin raised her hand and cut her short.

"No 'buts', my girl. I'll tell your mum and dad where you are and that you're safe with the nuns. Now pop upstairs and pack your bags. I'll take you to Killarney Street to meet the nuns right away."

Judy made her way upstairs, frantically considering which options she had other than running away. She packed her bags, concluding that she had no choice in the matter. After all, nuns must be kinder and more caring than Erin or Patrick could ever be. Or so she thought.

The Magdalene Laundries were scattered over Ireland, including Northern Ireland. The overwhelming factor in admissions to them was family pressure—anger, misery and disappointment at the discovery or revelation of a pregnancy. But these emotions were nothing compared to the embarrassment felt by these families, caused by judgement in the community. This was certainly true for Judy. Her parents had sent their daughter, finding her in a difficult position, away from home as if she did not exist. All to shield themselves from the embarrassment that their daughter might be seen as a harlot or a slut. Not once did they consider what was best for Judy or their unborn grandchild.

These laundries had nothing to do with 'saving fallen women'. They were money-making franchises for slave labour and baby farming.

Endless misery for the mothers, but also the children, all in exchange for money. The laundries themselves were a massive money spinner, too, as the women worked for their keep whilst the nuns took in laundry for handsome rewards. For Erin, it was a huge boost to her income, as she still collected money from her brother to look after Judy, whilst Judy worked for her keep at the laundry.

When they arrived at the laundry premises, Judy was introduced to the Mother Superior, who seemed quite warm and gentle, even though her face had a stern look. After a tour of the institution, including an introduction to the rules and the place where she would sleep, eat and work, Erin said,

"Right, thank you, Mother Superior. I'll be off now. You be good and work hard, Judy. I'll pop by from time to time to see how you're getting on."

With that, Erin left. The door banged, and Judy turned to face her new life—for the next 8 months, at least.

The Mods

Back at the Busy Bee Café, things continued as normal. Jimmy recovered from his accident in hospital. Jokerman assumed Jimmy's role as the de facto leader and arranged visits to the hospital on Jimmy's mum's request. Gerry continued with her hairdressing course. She missed Judy a great deal but knew she couldn't put her own life on hold. She eventually called round to see Judy, but her dad told her that Judy had gone to Ireland to live with her aunt and uncle. Gerry had no way of contacting Judy. Judy's dad told her to stay away and not to pester them anymore. Gerry was beside herself with grief at the loss of her best friend and regretted that she didn't go to see her earlier, perhaps the very next day, for an explanation.

Gerry's world came to a grinding halt when her dad made the announcement that her family would be moving back to Glasgow right after Christmas—"Before Hogmanay, if possible," her dad said.

She protested, but every reason for staying was met with resistance. She could find her own place—no, she was too young. She had her college courses to finish—no, she could continue her hairdressing course at the local college in Glasgow. She didn't dare tell her dad that she was in a serious relationship because she feared his anger and knew the January deadline would be pushed forward.

When she told Jokerman she was moving away, he was very upset. He vowed that he would continue their relationship, despite the distance between them. In the meantime, they agreed that Gerry would stay away from Busy Bee nights, rather than risk being caught out on the bike, like Judy had been. Their relationship was restricted to brief meetings in Watford's Cassiobury park, close to the college, which meant that romantic encounters were rare.

December weather made record night riding challenging, and the disastrous consequences of Jimmy's crash were still etched into everyone's mind.

A new phenomenon or cult sprang up. The Mods came to town.

The sixties were a decade defined by youth culture, and the Mods were at the forefront of it in Britain. With their sharp suits tailored to perfection and a sharp focus on fashion, music, and scooters, Mods represented a break from tradition and a celebration of modernity. The Mod movement wasn't just about appearance; it was a lifestyle. With bands like The Who and The Small Faces providing the soundtrack to their lives, Mods embraced a cosmopolitan approach to music and culture, looking to European trends for influence.

Central to Mod identity was the scooter—iconic machines like the Vespa and Lambretta became symbols of status and style. Mods would often be seen cruising around London and other cities, their scooters decorated with mirrors, lights and chrome, adding to the image of rebellion and sophistication. Their style wasn't just about clothes; it was about attitude, with a love for fast-paced city living and a desire to stand out in a world that was changing rapidly. Mods adopted the US Army parka as a badge signifying that they were mods. The green fishtail parka with a fur-lined hood, worn when riding their scooters, was an essential part of a mods' wardrobe.

The Mods and their motorbike-riding counterparts, The Rockers, were miles apart. The leather-jacketed bikers with swept-back hair held in place with Brylcreem were considered scruffy, even dirty. They were nicknamed 'Greasers', whereas anything stylish or cutting-edge could be described as 'Mod'. Their haircut and outfits made them feel like the most fashionable groups around. As such, Mods and Rockers were sworn enemies.

Jokerman and the gang were enjoying an evening at the Busy Bee one night early in December. Buddy Holly's song, 'Heartbeat', was ringing out of the jukebox as a bit of nostalgia when a Mod on a Vespa scooter rode into the bike park. It was raining hard, so everyone thought he was desperate for shelter—or just plain mad. When he walked into the café with his parka dripping wet, he looked up and suddenly realised where he was. The place went completely silent, apart from Buddy Holly singing 'Heartbeat'. The Mod thought better than turning to run; he made his way to the counter and nervously ordered a Pepsi. He sensed that the Rockers were encircling him at the bar. He froze but carried on drinking his Pepsi.

After ten minutes or so of very uncomfortable silence, he said, "All right, lads, a mucky night for riding, eh?"

He turned to leave, but the bikers crowded closer around him. Turd leaned forward, and standing on tiptoe, whispered in his ear, "You've got one minute to leave, and then we'll come after you. Got it?"

The mod nodded and ran out of the café. The bikers jeered and laughed.

Two seconds later, the Mod reappeared at the door.

"Where the fuck has my scooter gone?" he said, bewildered.

The Rockers shrugged their shoulders, laughing even louder. The police were called and took statements from everyone. Of course, nobody knew what had happened to the scooter. The Mod gave his name and address. The police assured him they would update him when they found the scooter.

A week later, Peter Turnball, who was over six feet tall but nicknamed 'Little Pete', answered his front door in Elstree. Two policemen stood on the doorstep.

"Mr Turnball, we have located your scooter. I can inform you it is now at a police compound ready for you to collect. You will need to bring your driving licence to show the police officers at the compound."

"Thank God for that," said Little Pete with some relief. "Which police compound? I'll collect it this morning."

The policemen were welling up inside. They looked at each other, then, trying his hardest not to laugh, one announced: "Aberystwyth in Wales,"

Christmas came and went. Gerry said an emotional goodbye to Jokerman. Both promised to keep in touch. She and her family moved back to Glasgow after nearly ten years in Radlett, Hertfordshire. Gerry wondered if she would ever see Jokerman again. She was still puzzled as to what had happened to her best friend, Judy. She had not seen nor heard from her since mid-October. It made her very sad, but she was also deeply concerned, for she had no idea why Judy had disappeared! She swore that she would keep in touch with Jokerman. If Judy reappeared at any time, he would let her know.

Towards the end of January, Jimmy came home to convalesce. His mum took time out of her own schedule to look after him. He had sustained a serious fracture to his right leg. It took two months and three operations to pin his right femur back together. The physiotherapy programme worked, and he was progressing well. Walking using crutches and anticipating that he would go back to work early in February, his mood was buoyant.

Whilst he had been away, the project he had been working hard to complete—the fighter jet project—was scrapped by the UK government. Jimmy's job was in jeopardy. However, that project was to be replaced by the Concorde project. A supersonic passenger jet plane that would cut the time to fly to the USA to just three hours. A joint venture project with the French government, it was anticipated that Concorde's maiden flight would take place before the end of the decade.

Jimmy hoped he would get onto the team of draughtsmen seconded from BSP to the project in Weybridge, Surrey, due to start by the end of March 1964.

The crash on the A41 had not dampened his passion for motorbikes. In fact, he was determined to use the scrap money from the sale of his wrecked Triumph 500cc Twin to a scrap dealer to help buy a new bike. He was a Triumph man through and through. He set his sights on the latest T120 650cc Triumph Bonneville. Despite protestations from his mum, who feared that her only son might die the next time he had an accident, he was determined to get a hire purchase agreement in place and buy the new bike by the end of March.

Jimmy took delivery of his new Bonneville early in April. With practice and rehabilitation, physio and a lot of hard work, he was walking without a limp and was looking forward to getting back to the Busy Bee to see all the old gang. He wanted to compare his new Bonneville to Grumpy's older 650 cc. He hoped that his new bike did not leak oil like Grumpy's did.

Meanwhile, over in Ireland, Judy was just over six months pregnant, and it showed. She endured her time at the Magdalene Laundry. Exhausted, she did the work, which was never-ending; day in and day out, washing and ironing, spending long days permanently on her feet. She saw her aunt once a month and was sincerely assured that Erin had been in touch with her parents regularly, and they were comforted that she was safe and well. Surviving the laundry ordeal was turning out to be just bearable, mainly due to her friendship with Caitlin, an Irish girl from a small village called Saggart, just west of Dublin. Caitlin was the same age as Judy and had also been banished by her parents to the Magdalene Laundry to save embarrassment at home.

Caitlin was also a little more than six months pregnant, so the two girls often discussed their fates. Neither had seen nor heard directly from their parents since they arrived at the laundry. At the beginning of their stay, both shared with each other that they were determined to keep their babies. But, as time went by, they witnessed other girls giving birth and watched their torment as the babies were immediately removed from the poor, wretched mothers. Judy and Caitlin concluded that the nuns were in charge, and the mothers could have no say in the outcome. Every week, they watched as a happy couple arrived at the chapel and then left with their newly adopted baby. Nobody knew what sort of transaction was taking place, but many suspected that substantial amounts of money were involved.

Judy told Caitlin that she had ambitions to be a hairdresser and to own her own business one day. She still harboured those ambitions. Although it would be heartbreaking to see her baby go, she decided it would be best if she could just remain silent, accept her fate, go back home to England to her parents' home and get on with her life as best she could. Caitlin agreed that that was the best course of action for Judy, but she feared that, for her, she would return to her village as a tarnished woman and end up a lonely spinster, shunned by the community. Judy tried all she could to inspire Caitlin to believe in herself, form dreams and work hard to fulfil those dreams. But it was clear that in a small Catholic village in Ireland, it would be very much harder than it would be for Judy, back in England. Or so Judy assumed.

Wednesday 10th June 1964

Judy woke early. Her bladder seemed full to almost bursting, and she waddled to the toilet. She'd had a terrible night of stomach cramps and back pain. She had just dropped off to sleep when her bladder decided it was full and that it was time to wake up and empty it. On the way to the toilet down the hall, a cramp in her stomach made her double over with the sudden ferocity of it. She groaned and leaned forward, holding on to the wall for support. The pain slowly started to abate, and she stood up again to gingerly make her way to the toilet. Judy realised that she hadn't been able to hold her pee and felt a gush of warmth down her legs.

'That's a lot of pee,' she thought, and then realised what had happened.

"Oh my God," she whispered. "It's happening. My baby's coming."

Her voice climbed in volume, and she waddled the rest of the way to the bathroom. A nun followed her down the hall and knocked on the door. She didn't wait for an answer but pushed open the door and walked right in.

"Stop that shouting," she said. "There are other people in the house, and they need their rest. They don't want to be listening to your racket."

Judy was taken to the birthing room, protesting that the baby must be early. She was not given time to say anything to Caitlin. "Have you had regular contractions yet?" One of the three nuns surrounding Judy asked. Judy shook her head. "I don't know. I was awake most of the night with backache and cramps..."

Another wave of pain washed over her, and she screwed her eyes tight and held her breath.

"My God. Ahh—that hurts!" she grunted through gritted teeth.

"Don't blaspheme, my girl; this is punishment for your loose ways."

Mother Superior watched over the proceedings as other nuns administered to the panicking Judy. She had no idea what to expect. No one had told her, and she lay on the birthing bed worrying about the conversation she had overheard between her parents the day she found out why she was an only child.

She grasped the sleeve of the Mother Superior.

"Am I going to be all right? I'm... I'm not going to die, am I? My baby won't die?"

Mother Superior's response was not comforting. "It sometimes happens that one or both should die, but it is God's will, and we accept the dangers. It's the payment for your promiscuity. Now, stop your yelling and concentrate on delivering this baby."

With no support or sympathy, and certainly no pain relief, Judy did as she was told for the benefit of her new baby. She pushed with all her strength when they told her to, and for her efforts, received the most unimaginable pain in return. When, at last, the wail of her newborn rang out, she gave a sigh of utter relief and allowed her head to lower to the bed.

"Can I see my baby, please?" she asked. "Just for a moment?"

"It's a baby girl, and no, you can't see her," the Mother Superior said in a stern voice. "It's better for all concerned if you don't."

Judy believed the birth itself would be the most pain she could experience until she realised the baby was no longer hers. The child she had spoken to as she developed inside her, sang lullabies to, and who had responded to her voice and her touch whenever Judy could devote the time to getting to know her baby, was gone. She was someone else's child now. Judy would never see her first steps, hear her first words, or nurse scrapes and sorrows. That realisation cut Judy's heart like a red-hot blade.

"I'll never forgive any of them," she whispered in her bed that night as she sobbed herself to sleep. "Not one, not my mum or dad, and not that ruddy jealous cow, Erin. As for Patrick, he can just go to hell, too!"

Caitlin had her baby a few days later and went through the same process of never getting a chance to see the baby boy that had been born to her. Just over a week later, both girls left the laundry to face their individual futures but without any knowledge of what happened to their babies. It was an efficient and brutal process, administered by nuns acting on behalf of God whilst profiteering for the church.

Friday 19th June 1964

Erin stood waiting for Judy when she left the Magdalene Laundry. They walked together, back to Beaver Close. When they got to the kitchen, Erin turned to Judy. "Right, Judy, now that's over with, you can start again, rebuild your life and try to stay out of trouble. Your Ma and Da will be here tomorrow to take you home on Sunday. I've told them about the Magdalene laundry. They understand that it was best for you to be there. Now, you stay away from my Patrick when he comes home. In the meantime, you can clean up the kitchen for me, please."

'Blimey,' thought Judy. 'The bitch said please!' Erin made no reference to the baby; she behaved as if it never happened. Judy steeled herself in anticipation of seeing her parents for the first time since they dumped her in Ireland all those months ago. Judy recalled the night after the birth of her daughter, the misery and physical pain she had endured and the discomfort she still endured. The process of her milk drying up was uncomfortable and, at times, torture. Her breasts felt hard and swollen, and if she forgot about their tenderness and bumped them, the flare of fresh agony ripped through her chest all over again.

She also remembered the promise she'd made that night, that she would never forget or forgive those who had abandoned her when she needed them most. She could understand Erin's mercenary ideals to an extent—the woman had nothing in the way of wealth, especially when she compared Erin's life to her own—but her own parents? Her own mother? Judy knew that she would have fought harder for her child, and, therefore, her mother should have fought harder for Judy's interests, especially when she knew firsthand the dangers she faced.

Judy had changed everything about herself. She had grown from a young girl to a woman with strong ideals for herself and the ones she cared about. She decided that she would return to her home with her parents on her own terms. They would either like it or lump it.

Saturday 20th June 1964

Jack and Mary McDermott arrived just after lunch. They caught the early sailing from Holyhead that morning. Mary, tears flowing, rushed out of the car to hug her daughter at the gate. Judy tried to show her mother the same level of affection, but, somehow, she couldn't manage it. Raw, painful memories of the ordeal Judy had been through meant something had been lost, and she no longer felt the same way about her parents as she once had. She had tried to persuade herself that she was looking forward to seeing them again and returning home, but she remembered the lack of contact and the visits they could have made yet didn't, and she felt abandoned. Barely returning the hug to her mum, Judy only nodded to her father, then she went inside and upstairs to her room.

"She'll come round. Don't worry," said Erin, smiling at Jack and Mary.

Patrick appeared and said, "Come on Jack, put your overnight bags in the hall. We can nip to the pub for a few pints before supper."

Off went the two men, leaving Erin and Mary in the kitchen to prepare supper and exchange pleasantries.

Judy did not speak at the supper table. She listened to their conversation; they were all avoiding the obvious, and she noticed that at least her mother had the decency to be embarrassed. After they ate, Judy cleared the table, washed everything up and went to her room without saying goodnight.

The next morning, the fractured family left after breakfast to make the long journey back to Letchmore Heath. Jack and Mary tried to engage their daughter in conversation, but after a few one-word responses and Judy ignoring other questions altogether, they gave up. Jack drove back home in a darkening mood, and Mary became more morose as they travelled. Both wondered if they had done the right thing.

Judy spent the first week at home in self-imposed isolation in her room. She found out that Gerry had moved to Glasgow, but very little else. She visited Radlett village and spoke to the manager at Bishop's supermarket who, remembering how good she was on the delicatessen counter, gave her a full-time job for the summer. She started work on Monday, 29th June, and everyone welcomed her back as if she had never been away.

The new phenomenon, which was starting to emerge on the youth scene, caught her attention. The Mods were making their presence heard. She had been reading about the Mods and liked what she saw. Everything from the fashions—short-cropped hair for the girls and tidy, styled hair for the boys, short skirts, parka coats, scooters and the fast beat of their pop music—fascinated Judy. Before starting work at Bishop's, she had her hair cropped short and revamped her makeup, making sure to wear plenty of eye makeup. She did her best to try to shut the old Judy out of her mind. 'A new look for a new Judy', she thought to herself. A fleeting thought of Jimmy brought back every terrible memory of that autumn through to that summer in Ireland, and she would rather not be reminded of any of it. She was determined to reinvent herself and attack life head-on.

New Life, New name

Saturday July 11th 1964

Jess King finished work early. It wasn't unusual for him to work on a Saturday; it was all useful overtime money. He was an apprentice toolmaker at Handley Page's aeroplane factory in Park Street. Every day, he rode his Lambretta GT200 to work from his home in Leaming Road, Borehamwood. His GT200 was British Racing green, had the letter J on the front with chrome side panels that gleamed in the sun, a red flyscreen, copious amounts of lights, mirrors, a steel sprung backrest for pillion passengers and an enormous aerial at the back with a faux fox's tail hanging from the top. This particular Saturday, he pulled up in Radlett outside Bishop's supermarket to buy some cigarettes. Before leaving, he decided to sit on his scooter, enjoying a fag before heading home.

Jess was eighteen and chose to be an apprentice despite being academically bright, with good grades in his A-levels from the grammar school in Borehamwood. Earning money would give him the opportunity to train in something practical whilst financing his passion for all things Mod. His parka was covered in old military badges—mostly American—and he had a large RAF roundel applied to the back. Had he not opted for an apprenticeship, he would have almost certainly gone to university and studied law. But that ambition could wait. He had decided that enjoying his teenage years and funding his passion, particularly his beloved scooter, was more important at this stage of his life.

He was just finishing his cigarette when a fabulous-looking girl complete with a mod hairstyle came out of Bishop's supermarket and proceeded to cross the service road right in front of him. Jess was taken aback by how attractive the girl was, and he immediately went into pickup mode.

"Hello, gorgeous. Where have you been all my life?" swooned Jess with his best smile.

Judy found herself surprisingly receptive to this first bit of flirting so soon after her dreadful ordeal in Ireland. The boy in front of her sat astride his gleaming scooter; he had a cheeky grin, a cute face, gorgeous icy blue eyes and a strange, almost girly hairstyle with a central parting encircling his face. She found the combination, coupled with his smart appearance, very attractive.

"Who wants to know?" she shot back with an encouraging smile.

"You tell me your name first, and then I'll tell you mine," teased Jess.

"OK, that's easy. My name is Judy. Now, what's your name?"

"I don't believe it," said Jess, trying to look shocked but pleased at the same time. He threw back his head and looked to the sky. "It must be fate that we have met." He had his hands clasped to his heart, cuddling himself affectionately. "Look, I have a J for Judy on the front of my scooter. We were meant to meet—it's our destiny."

He knew it was a bit corny, but, surprisingly, it seemed to be working. Judy was smiling back at his theatrics; she clearly liked this cheeky, cocky guy.

"OK, very good. You can cut the corny chat now. What's your name? I told you mine." Judy had her hands on her hips in a pose that said: 'come on then, out with it now; my patience is wearing thin'.

Quick thinking was required, as he had boxed himself into a difficult position. Admitting that his real name was Jess would just wreck the chat-up line about having a J on the front of his scooter completely. He leaned back and folded his arms in a proud stance.

"Terry. That's my name," he said. He smiled broadly, believing that he was making headway with this girl.

"OK, Terry, I'm off to catch my bus home. Nice to have met you," Judy laughed and went to move on.

"No, no, no—wait! Where are you going? We've only just met—I can give you a lift. Please let me take you home," Jess, now known to her as Terry, stammered as he pleaded with her to keep the conversation going. He decided then and there to keep up the charade about his name—he would have to handle that problem later. The important thing was to get this fish on the hook right now. Taking on an expression that was vacant and lost, his eyes were urging her to consider him giving her a lift home.

Tutting, shrugging her shoulders dismissively, Judy looked to the sky and said, "Well, OK. Thanks, Terry. I live in Letchmore Heath—you can drop me off outside the Three Horseshoes Pub."

She climbed on to the back of his scooter. Jess thought she must have ridden pillion before, given her confidence in mounting his scooter.

"Great. Sit tight, gorgeous; the Three Horseshoes pub it is, then," replied the very happy lad.

They exited the service road onto Watling Street, then went left up Aldenham Avenue. Jess knew the way to Letchmore Heath. Judy leant on the backrest, which bent slightly as he accelerated up the hill, sending a familiar shiver up her spine. This was a very different experience from riding pillion on the back of a motorbike. She did not need to hold onto the rider, as her feet were on running boards. It was altogether more comfortable; now, she could fold her arms, lean back and observe the scenery.

Terry had not given her any safety instructions like Jimmy had when she first rode on the back of his bike. Content with how safe she felt, she relaxed and enjoyed the ride.

It was a lovely sunny evening when they pulled up outside the Three Horseshoes pub. People had started to arrive at the pub just as it was opening. Parents left their children outside at wooden tables as they went inside to order drinks. Coca-Cola bottles with straws and packets of Smiths crisps were deposited in front of kids whilst their parents enjoyed a drink inside. The kids took great delight in untwisting the small blue bag found in the Smiths crisp bag and sprinkling the salt contents onto the crisps.

"Fancy a night out with me? Some of my mates and their girlfriends are going to Watford later, to the Trade Club. The Who are playing. They're a new band—I'm sure they're destined for fame. What do you say? Why don't you join us? It will be a fun Saturday night out. I can pick you up here at 7pm." He was not concerned that he appeared overly keen or even pleading.

She was a great catch—he was smitten already.
Putting her finger to her lips, Judy looked to the sky long enough to tease him and keep him waiting.

"OK," she said after a moment, "I'll be here at seven pm."

She smiled, turned and skipped off round the corner to her house. When she got home, she announced that she was going out that night on the back of a scooter to the Trade Club in Watford. She had resolved not to hide any secrets from her parents again. She had made it clear that after the ordeal endured in Ireland, she would not be told what she could and could not do. Her parents recognised that they had little alternative but to accept the situation.

The Trade Club in Watford was based at the Trade Union Hall at the junction of Woodford and Clarendon roads. It was the place to be on a Saturday night if you were a Mod. The hall held a thousand people, and live bands played every Friday and Saturday night. Another local trendy place was the Linx club in Borehamwood, which freely advertised that scooters and parkas were welcome. Both clubs attracted up-and-coming rock and pop bands from the surrounding area. They were widely recognised as incubator clubs for bands breaking into the London scene. Next stop, the big time.

After tea, Judy got herself ready for the night ahead, making an effort to wear everything mod: a pinafore dress that ended just above the knee, square-toed shoes with a short square heel, sensitive light eye makeup and her cropped hair standing up on her head held in place with hairspray. She inspected her look in the mirror and winked but acknowledged to herself that she was not ready for romance. It was too early, and she just wanted to have a good time.

Jess could not believe his luck. He grinned as he rode home, excited at the prospect of the night ahead. Judy had left her mark on his emotions, and she was foremost in his thoughts. He ran indoors and scoffed down his supper, then went to his room to get ready. Earlier that day, he had been full of anticipation for a wild night. The Who were a newly formed band with a reputation for aggressive playing and generally creating mayhem. After meeting Judy that afternoon, his mind was in turmoil. He thought that she was stunning. Following just a brief encounter, he knew that there was something special about this girl.

At five feet eleven, Jess was average in size. He had mousy brown hair that was backcombed on the top with a centre parting but was longer than his parents liked—especially his dad, who often referred to him as a girl. He checked himself out in the mirror, smoothed his hair at the side and winked one of his ice-blue eyes, knowing that he was dressed to impress the skirts. Strangely, he didn't need to do that now. Only Judy needed to be impressed.

He completed his dark blue mohair suit by putting on his jacket, straightening his one-inch-wide tie and donning his parka.

He ran downstairs yelling, "Bye, mum! Bye, Dad! I'll be home by midnight."

He kick-started his scooter, put on most of his lights and set off towards Theobold Street, making quite a racket from his big bore exhaust. Then he turned right towards Radlett to meet up with his mates.

He was first to arrive at the layby outside the post office in Radlett, where they had arranged to meet. He heard Nester before he saw him on his Lambretta GT200, which had been bored out to

225 cc. Nester's big-bore exhaust was louder than Jess's; the two-stroke engine went pop, pop, pop, pop with a deafening cry when decelerating through the gears. Nester pulled in, taking off his 'pork pie' hat that was pulled down over his eyes to save it from blowing off during riding.

Nester was Danny Ottway's nickname. He and Jess had been friends since they were seven years old. When they were young in the 1950s, they regularly went bird's nesting together in the springtime, collecting eggs, blowing the yolk and keeping the perfectly formed shells on straw carefully labelled to identify the species. In fact, Nester got his nickname from his childhood mate who, together with Jess, formed a threesome to go bird's nesting. Nester had also given his mate his nickname. It was Turd. Steve Wright, shite, or Turd. Nester was now a Mod and Turd a Rocker, so they had seen less of each other since they had become teenagers. The only contact they had had was to nod to one another.

Nester was the best at collecting eggs, hence his nickname, but Turd was fearless when it came to climbing trees. Jess often told the story of the time the three of them, just ten years old, found a crow's nest at the top of an enormous oak tree. The only way to get the eggs was for one of them to climb to the top, another to climb two-thirds up, and the last one to climb a third of the way up. Turd got to the top of the tree, at least fifty feet in the air. There were three eggs. Perfect. Taking one, he put it in his mouth and took it down to Nester, who, in turn, put it in his mouth and took it down to Jess, who put it in his mouth and took it to the ground. They repeated this exercise three times. When Turd got to the nest for the third time, both the crows returned, squawking loudly. They proceeded to dive-bomb Turd at the nest. He brushed them aside, took the last egg and descended to the ground with Nester protecting him from the distressed birds. Two of the eggs had already formed chicks, so they couldn't be blown. The third egg was OK, and the yolk blew through the pinhole. The other two eggs, they threw away. They all agreed that Turd would keep the blown egg, as he had climbed to the very top of the tree. It was something they would regret later in life, but bird nesting was common amongst young boys in the fifties.

Once they had all gone through puberty and reached their mid-teens, Nester retained his nickname for a different type of nesting other than bird's nesting.

"You OK, Jess?" shot Nester as he pulled in and put his scooter on the stand. "Looking forward to a good night out at the Trade? It should be good—everyone's saying The Who are going to have hit records one day."

"Yeah," replied Jess, "let's hope that they continue to play the Trade if they become famous. Anyway, you'll never guess what! I've had a very productive afternoon. Just by chance, I stopped on my way home from work for a fag outside Bishop's just over there. A gorgeous girl walked right in front of my scooter. After some classy chat-up lines, she agreed to join us tonight. I'm picking her up in Letchmore Heath at 7 pm."

"Well done, mate. You'd better get going then. I'll wait here for the others. We'll meet you at Round Bush at about ten past seven," said Nester with a wink.

Jess nodded and rode off to pick up Judy.

Shortly afterwards, Mick Alder arrived on his Lambretta LI 150 cc. Mick's nickname was Shadow, as he always seemed to appear from nowhere. Jim Williams followed up on his Vespa 200 cc. Jim's nickname was Yankee because he was American; his father was the vice president of Coca-Cola UK. They lived in Northwood. Jim was staying with Mick the Shadow for the weekend.

Two girls, Julie Cassidy and Jackie Owens, turned up. Both lived in Radlett.

"Hi, guys," they said. "Are you ready to go?"

"Yep, hop on. We're meeting Jess at Round Bush, and little Pete will meet us at the Trade Club," called out Nester. Jackie climbed on the back of Nester's scooter whilst Julie got on the back with Yankee. The three scooters set off up Aldenham Road, then on to the Watford Road. Next stop, Round Bush.

Jess pulled up outside the Three Horseshoes, put his scooter on the stand, lit up a fag and waited for Judy. When Judy rounded the corner, he caught sight of her in her black plastic coat, looking every bit a Mod. He felt a tingling in his spine that he had not felt about any girl before. He took one last drag on his fag and flicked the butt away, blowing the smoke high into the sky.

"Hello, Judy. You look gorgeous! My mates will meet us at Round Bush at ten past seven, but before we meet them, I have a confession to make."

'Oh no', thought Judy, 'he's married or something. Shame, because he is very cute. I could really fancy him'.

He went on, "My name isn't Terry. It's Jess. I thought you should know before we meet my mates."

Almost breaking up with laughter inside, Judy folded her arms and put on a very stern face.

"Well, well—that's why there is a J on the front of your scooter! It's nothing to do with destiny at all," she said mockingly, clutching her heart and looking skyward as Jess had earlier. "Well, that's your problem because from now on, you will always be Terry to me. Better tell your mates that when we see them."

With that, she laughed and climbed on the back of his scooter.

They moved off to Round Bush, where the others were waiting in the layby. When they pulled in to meet them, Nester signalled to get going.

Jess waved his hand.

"No. Wait, guys. Let's do some introductions first," he said. "

Everyone, this beauty on the back is Judy, who I met earlier today."

They all nodded towards Judy.

Nester shouted, "Welcome, Judy. Good to have you in the gang—should be a fun night."

Jess started the introductions.

"Judy, this is Nester. I've known him all my life. His real name is Danny, but I'll explain his nickname later. Behind Nester is

Jackie. And this is Mick, known as Shadow because he always seems to appear from nowhere. This is Jim, known as Yankee because he is a yank, and behind him is Julie. OK, those are the introductions done. Let's go and see The Who."

"Oh no, wait up just a minute," shouted Judy, putting her hand in the air, "aren't you forgetting to introduce yourself, Terry?"

She was laughing loudly.

"OK, OK, OK. Fair enough. Guys, this afternoon I conned Judy into believing that my name was Terry, and now she is refusing to call me anything else," confessed Jess.
"No problem, Terry," said Nester as he pulled away with a wink and a smile.

"All right, Tel," laughed Shadow as he passed.

"Come on—keep up, Terry!" shouted Yankee as he sped off with Julie laughing out loud.

Jess locked into first gear and rode after them, wondering how long this would last.

"Satisfied?" he yelled back at Judy.

"Yes, thanks, Terry," was the response. Little did Jess know that he would become known as Terry for the rest of his life.

Judging by how many scooters were parked up close by, the Trade Club was buzzing. They found a place to pull in and were promptly joined by Little Pete, who was in fact over six feet tall.

"Alright, Little Pete," shouted Nester, "better leave your scooter close to ours. Don't want it to end up in Wales again."

Everyone laughed.

"Fuck off," responded little Pete. "That joke is wearing a bit thin now, guys."

Inside the Trade Club, the place was rocking. A record was blaring out; it was Lulu and the Lovers screaming, *'Shout, come on now, don't forget to say you will, don't forget to shout now, ah shout, shout, shout...'* The air was thick with cigarette smoke. The different outfits on display made for a colourful scene. Judy couldn't help thinking how different all the guys looked compared to the Rockers at the Busy Bee, who all looked the same.

As Lulu finished, the DJ played 'Walk on By' by Dionne Warwick. Suddenly, boys and girls were dancing close together to the romantic melody.

Terry, as he was now known, took Judy in his arms, gently swaying to the music. Judy was impressed with his smart appearance, cute hairstyle and icy blue eyes. She smiled, and he leaned forward to kiss her. Her rejection was abrupt. It even surprised her. Was it too soon for just a kiss? Her breasts were still painful as her milk had only just dried up. Confused, her head was spinning; he was cute, he didn't deserve her reaction. It seemed to be just instinct at that moment.

"I'm, er, I'm sorry. I've just finished with a long-term boyfriend," she lied. "I'm still a bit emotional, sorry."

Looking concerned, he nodded, cuddling her affectionately.

"That's OK," he whispered in her ear, "I fancy you rotten. We can take as long as you want. I'll wait forever for my first kiss."

His cheeky response was also strangely sincere. She smiled back, nodding.

"I fancy you too. Just let's take it slowly."

He squeezed her tightly.

"Fine by me."

The record finished; the atmosphere changed as the crowd anticipated the energy that was just about to begin. The compere announced, "Everyone please welcome to the stage an exciting new group of local lads. Please give a Trade Club welcome to The Who."

The place erupted with shouts, cheers and screams as Pete Townsend, Roger Daltrey, Keith Moon and John Entwistle ran onto the stage. They started with 'Zoot Suit', their first record: "*I'm the hippiest number in town, and I'll tell you why—I'll tell you why. I'm the snappiest dresser right now, to my inch-wide tie, inch-wide tie...*" rang out Roger Daltry's voice.

The crowd was jumping in the air with an energy not normally seen in dance halls. At the end of the number, Pete Townsend went to the mike.

"Thank you. It's great to be here. Our manager has changed our name to the High Numbers; that was our first release. But everyone, including the compere here, seems to recognise us as The Who." He then stepped back, shouting, "One, two, three, four!"

He flayed his arm like a windmill struck his guitar. Everyone started jumping to *The* 'Summertime Blues'.

The sight of bouncing teenagers all jumping in the air was quite amazing. Judy thought that this was much more fun than the Busy Bee nights and the pinball machines. She could not believe the excitement generated by the band. The drummer was clearly quite mad, hitting the instrument at a ferocious speed; the singer spun his mike on its wire above his head; the guitarist seemed to be able to leap in the air whilst still playing while the other guitarist stayed still and expressionless.

Judy and all the others were buzzing with energy by the end of the evening. Most had sweat dripping from their hair, but nobody cared. Once the band had played three encores, they eventually left the stage to cries of:

"More! More! More!"

Leaving the Trade Club, they made their way back to the scooters. Both Shadow and Little Pete had chatted up girls in the club.

"This is Gill. I'm taking her back to Borehamwood," said Shadow.

"And this is Carol. I'm taking her home to Garston," revealed little Pete.

All the couples got on to their scooters and set off on the separate journeys home.

It was 11.30pm when Terry cruised his scooter from Round Bush down to Letchmore Heath to drop Judy home. He pulled up outside the Three Horseshoes. She got off the scooter and turned to him. She smiled, fluttering her eyelids in a way that almost melted Terry's heart.

"I'm sorry about earlier," she whispered in his ear.

Then, gently, she kissed him on the lips. It was a slow, gentle kiss at first, but it deepened, eventually resulting in tongues softly touching. As she backed away, Terry took a deep breath.

"Well, that was worth waiting for. Can I see you again? I hope there will be more of those to come."

"I'd like that," replied Judy. They agreed to meet the following week for a cinema date. Thus began a slow-burn romance that grew into something that would last a very long time.

For the rest of the summer, the group of Mods met regularly. They enjoyed ride-outs to Clacton-on-Sea, Brighton and Bournemouth. 'Can't buy me Love' was a huge hit for the Beatles, as was 'Have I the Right' by the Honeycombs and 'A World Without Love' by Peter and Gordon, amongst other songs released that spelt the beginning of the swinging sixties.

The Marquee Club, Love on the train

Eight Months Later End of March 1965

Judy had started her hairdressing course again, but quickly decided that she enjoyed working at the Bishop's Supermarket. She had become the most dependable Saturday and holiday worker that the manager had to call upon. The manager, Mr Gain, talked to his area manager and agreed to offer Judy a full-time management trainee position starting as provisions manager at the Radlett branch. Judy explained her decision to her mum and dad. In April 1965, she left the hairdressing course at Cassio College and started with Bishop's, recognising that she might be asked to work at any branch from time to time or even at the head office in South Ruislip, Middlesex.

Terry had re-evaluated his career. His A-level results from the last year at school were enough to allow him to register to go to university to study law in September later that year. He and Judy had expressed ambitious plans together: Judy would go into supermarkets and Terry into law. They were even talking about a future together, despite the fact that their physical relationship was limited to kissing and fondling. Terry said he could wait for a more serious relationship, pledging his love for Judy regularly. Judy had grown very fond of Terry. He was funny, handsome, kind and head over heels in love with her.

They were very much an item and had been going out together for eight months. Nester and Jackie had also settled into a long-term relationship. The four of them frequented the Linx Club in Borehamwood and the Trade Club in Watford, seeing bands like The Small Faces, Georgie Fame and The Blue Flames and, of course, The Who. The Who had released their first hit, 'Can't Explain', which had appeared on the new TV show, Ready Steady Go. 'Can't Explain' reached number 8 in the UK singles chart.

It was Nester who suggested that the four of them book a holiday in the summer at a holiday camp. They found one at Littlestone-on-Sea on the south coast near the Romney Marshes. It was a Maddisons Holiday Camp. It was quite small, and they would have a chalet for each couple. They booked it for the last week of May.

That gave Judy three months to prepare for a romantic week with Terry. She told her parents about the holiday. By now, they had met Terry and had come to terms with Judy riding on the back of a scooter but still expressed concern that she had no crash helmet.

Tuesday March 16th 1965

Judy had arranged for her day off that week to fall on Wednesday so that she could lay in, because it was the night before they were going to the Marquee Club in Soho to see The Who. The whole gang had tickets: Terry, Judy, Nester, Jackie, Shadow, Gill, Yankee, Julie, Little Pete and Carol. They decided to get the train from Radlett, or, for some, Borehamwood, to St Pancras, then underground to Oxford Circus, where they would go on to talk to The Marquee in Wardour Street. The Marquee didn't have a licence to serve alcohol, but there was a bar close by called La Chasse. Since most of the gang had arranged a day off the next day, they all decided they would go on a bender.

A night out in London meant showing off one's fashion sense and being as Mod as possible. Judy had obtained a black-and-white diamond-shaped checkered pinafore dress, white knee-high boots and a black leather coat complete with a tie belt. With her cropped brown hair, dark eye makeup and rouge to emphasise her high cheekbones, she looked stunning. Her dad dropped her at Radlett station.

"Have a nice time, love," he smiled. "It's so good to see you enjoying life. Terry seems such a nice boy."

"Thanks, Dad. I'll be on the last train back tonight. Thanks for picking me up," replied, Judy.

Getting out of the car, she thought to herself, 'it's a pity that you didn't put me and your lost granddaughter before your embarrassment last year.'

Nester rolled up at the station with Jackie. He was wearing a black mohair suit, a black shirt and a one-inch white tie. Jackie had a short, straight black skirt, knee-high black boots and a multi-coloured striped sweater, with a red ribbon tying up her buffoon hair complete with kiss curls. Yankee, Julie, Shadow and Gill all pitched up on time looking equally mod. There was not a parka in sight, as they were generally only for riding on the scooter.

"OK, we are all here. Terry, Little Pete and Carol are getting on the train at Borehamwood. Let's go to platform one and get the 6.15pm train," explained Nester. They went over the footbridge to platform one. Radlett station was a charming station with flower boxes attached to the lovely stone buildings. It frequently won station of the year at that time.

The train was on time, and they had a carriage to themselves. As the train pulled into Borehamwood, Nester stuck his head out of the window and waved to Terry, Little Pete and Carol. They clambered onto the train. Terry had pushed the boat out with his fashion. His hair was a little longer now; it was heavily backcombed on the top with a centre parting that looked like curtains surrounding his face. He wore straight maroon trousers with a white leather belt, square-toed slip-on moccasin-shaped shoes, a red and white checked shirt, a one-inch red tie and a dark blue mohair jacket. As he entered the carriage with the sun low in the sky behind him, Judy looked up. For some reason, her heart jumped for a second. They had been together for eight months. She was fond of Terry, but in that split second, she felt like she was falling in love.

They arrived in Soho early and decided to grab a coffee at Le Macabre, which was just around the corner from the Marquee Club. It was an interesting coffee house; customers sat on black coffins, tipping ash into candlelit skulls and listening to funereal music on the jukebox. The tar-coloured walls were adorned with plastic skeletons, painted cobwebs and frescoes of naked women twirled in the moonlight by libidinous ghouls.

They all sat on chairs pulled up to the coffin tables and ordered coffee.

"Blimey. Never been this close to a coffin before," said Nester, feigning a shiver. They all laughed.

The group lit up fags and started talking about the night ahead. The Who had released their latest hit, 'My Generation'. It was fast, furious and summed up the mood of the Mods at the time.

They sang words like 'People try to put us down just because we get around. Things, they do look awful cold—hope I die before I get old. Talking 'bout my generation, baby.

Terry pondered, "I've been thinking about the words ever since the record came out. I think it means that we should not want to die young in years but die before we become old mentally."

"Fuck me, Terry, mate, that's all a bit deep on a night out. Pop a pill and go for a ride," exclaimed Nester with a smile as he took out a purple heart pill, shoved it in his mouth and swigged it down with coffee. A purple heart pill was known as an 'upper'; it gave you energy and kept you awake. It had been used in the war to enable soldiers to keep pushing through for longer periods in battle.

All the boys took one. The girls refrained, preferring to get high on the energy from the show. It was nearly time to go to the Marquee, with just enough time to stop by the bar La Chasse. The boys drank beer, and the girls, gin and orange.

The inside of the Marquee was packed with teenagers in mod gear all anticipating a great show. It was very cramped; the cigarette smoke hung in the air, and people were jostling for a position as close to the stage as possible. Then the DJ put on 'Go Now' by the Moody Blues, which had been released just before Christmas in 1964. The recording was done in a homemade studio in a garage at the back of the Marquee Club. It had shot to number one in the UK charts, putting the Moody Blues firmly on the map. Boys took their girls in their arms and smooched to this classic rock ballad.

"Happy?" Terry whispered in Judy's ear as they danced close together.

"Very, but I wish you wouldn't pop those pills. I love you just the way you are!"

'Blimey', thought Terry, 'that's the first time she has mentioned love'. He leaned forward, kissing her long and hard, oblivious to everyone else in the house.

"You'd better go now," the song finished.

The DJ shouted into the PA system, "Ladies and gentlemen, put your hands together for the Who!"

The place erupted in screams and shouts. The band ran onto the stage and kicked off with their first hit, 'Can't Explain'. The floor seemed to move as everybody jumped up and down. The energy was electric—quite different from other concerts at the time where the dancing was way more controlled and sedate. At the end of the number, they immediately swung into another of their singles, 'Anyway, Anyhow, Anywhere'.

The band was in full flow. Pete Townsend was strumming his guitar with a windmill action and leaping in the air; Roger Daltrey swung his mike like a lasso, catching it in perfect timing to sing his next line; and Keith Moon was a frantic drummer who looked like he just wanted to beat his drum kit to death. All this incredible energy seemed oblivious to John Entwistle, who stood almost motionless but ran his fingers up and down the neck of his bass guitar to keep up with Moon's frantic drumming. The crowd bounced around in unison, shaking their heads wildly.

At the end of the set, Pete Townsend leaned forward to the mike and announced, "Now for our latest hit: 'My Generation.'"

He stepped back and banged his guitar: dung, dung, dung, dung, dung, dung, dung, dung, dung.

"People try to put us d-d-dow, just because we get around. Things they do look awful c-c-c-cold—I hope I die before I get old," screamed Roger Daltrey, deliberately stuttering at the start of each line. Judy was jumping around and shaking her head like she had never done before, matched only by Terry doing the same crazy dance. The set ended with 'My Generation' as an encore straight after it had just been played.

They were buzzing, high on the energy from the show, as they left the Marquee to make their way back to St Pancras with just enough time to grab a couple of drinks at the La Chasse bar. A scuffle broke out between Shadow and some guy who had tried to come on to Gill in the club; he had followed them to the bar.

Nester stepped up, grabbing the guy by the throat, almost spitting angrily in his face as he spoke, "If you know what's good for you, you will piss off now. If not, I'll put your head through that window."

The guy was genuinely startled at the ferocity of Nester's action. Looking around, he saw he was on his own, so he thought better of it and scurried away.

They all laughed and carried on drinking, then headed back to St Pancras to catch the last train. Although they were still high from the Who, the kissing started as soon as they were all on the train.

Terry sensed that Judy had moved up a gear in her affection for him. It sent a tingle down his spine. They kissed hard as if they were the only people on the train as they trundled past Kentish Town. They found a compartment on their own, so Terry thought he could explore new territory. Their tongues were flicking back and forth, and Terry's hand was on Judy's knee. He ventured up her leg beyond the length of her skirt, past her stocking tops and suspenders, and into her crotch. He gently eased his hand inside her knickers, found her clitoris, and proceeded to masturbate her as affectionately as he knew how.

They went past West Hampstead station. Nobody came into their compartment. Judy, enjoying his tender touch, was starting to breathe heavily. This was the furthest they had been in eight months. She felt confident enough to run her hand up his leg to his belt, which she unbuckled, and slipped her hand into his underwear to find a very stiff penis, which she started to caress with enthusiasm. Their lips never seemed to part as all this masturbating was going on. Their kissing became more intense. They were both breathing heavily now. Cricklewood station went past in a blur. Still, they were alone.

As the rhythm of the train sped up, so did their movements on each other. They passed through Hendon station quicker and quicker. This was seriously good for them both. They were sweating with passionate excitement. As if by magic, they gasped, kissed hard and reached an orgasm at the same time. They flopped back onto the seat, looking at each other and mouthing, 'wow'. As the train pulled into Mill Hill Broadway, they had straightened up their clothing and were holding hands as a night worker got on the train and into their compartment.

Terry crossed his legs and put his other hand strategically across his lap to conceal any visible evidence of what may have passed between St Pancras and Mill Hill Broadway. They both smiled contentedly, as they felt that their relationship had moved on to new territory that evening. The train came to a stop in Borehamwood. Terry stood up, still a little embarrassed, kissed Judy and left with Little Pete and Carol.

Judy's dad was waiting at Radlett station to collect her. Nester, Jackie, Shadow, Gill, Yankee and Julie, who were staying within walking distance of the station, waved goodbye. The night was over.

Judy climbed into bed that night feeling good about her relationship with Terry. She felt more confident about the holiday they had booked for June that year, where they could move up another gear in comfortable surroundings. In fact, she was really looking forward to it now.

Retribution

Saturday 20th March 1965

Judy finished work at 5pm. Her dad was waiting outside Bishop's supermarket to take her home. After supper, she went upstairs to get ready for a night out at The Lynx Club in Borehamwood. Georgie Fame and The Blue Flames were playing, and she liked his music. It was more jazz/rock than pop. The Mods loved it. Her favourite was a song called 'Yeah, Yeah'. The memory of their last night out—'orgasms on the train', as she had nicknamed the event—brought a smile to her face.

She was falling deeper in love with Terry, so much so that she took Jimmy's ring from her right hand and put it in her drawer. That episode of her life was now well and truly over.

All the gang were going to the Lynx that night. Terry was picking her up from home at 6.45pm and then meeting the others outside the Post Office in Radlett at 7pm. Terry was now well and truly accepted by her mum and dad. He was a clever boy in their eyes, and although they disapproved of Judy riding on the back of his scooter, they accepted that there was nothing that they could say or do to stop it. Judy was ready on time, complete with a short black skirt, knee-high white boots, a multi-coloured knitted top and her parka complete with some new badges sewn on to the sleeves.

She had become used to her short hair, which meant she could be more elaborate with her eye makeup. It was the big attraction, rather than her hair. Cherry-red lipstick and her customary wink at herself in the mirror completed the preparation. She ran downstairs to find Terry in the lounge, deep in conversation with her mum and dad. 'This is getting a bit too cosy,' she thought to herself, smiling.

"Ready?" she asked. "We should be back by midnight. Don't wait up!"

She grabbed Terry by the hand and left as quickly as she could to avoid conversation.

As they decelerated through the gears down Aldenham Avenue to Radlett High Street, Terry's big bore exhaust made the familiar loud *pop, pop, pop* sound. They turned left to meet the others, who had already arrived. Terry nodded to them all as he pulled into the layby.

"Watcha, Terry," said Nester. "We've been chatting and thought we could go to the Lynx through Elstree via the A41 at Watford. If there aren't too many Greaser bikes at the Busy Bee, we could pull in, just to remind them that we have not forgotten what happened to Little Pete's scooter all those months ago. What do you think?"

Judy's heart missed a beat, but she was trying not to let it show. What if Jimmy and Jokerman were there? She had never explained her association with The Rockers, as it had felt like such a long time ago.

"Bloody good idea," Terry said enthusiastically. "Let's go."

He shot off, followed by the others, before Judy had time to say anything. She crossed her fingers and hoped that the Busy Bee bike park was full of bikes, deterring the boys from pulling in.

As they approached, she could see that there were only three bikes parked up. Her heart sank. 'Shit,' she thought. 'Is this the moment when my relationship with Terry is going to take a turn for the worse?' She recognised two of the bikes. One was Jokerman's, and the other belonged to Turd. The third bike was brand new, but because it was a Triumph, she had the dreadful thought that it might be Jimmy's.

Although the scooters were much less powerful than most big motorbikes, they made a hell of a racket and could be heard from a long way away. When they pulled into the bike park, two bikers emerged, walking towards them. It was Jokerman and Turd. The Mods kept their engines running.

Turd nodded at Nester and Terry. Judy assumed that they knew one another.

 "Alright, Nester. Alright, Jess. What the fuck do you think you are doing riding in here? This is our manor," said Turd fiercely. Judy thought that he clearly knew who they were.

"Good, thanks, Turd. By the way, he's known as Terry these days," Nester said, nodding towards his mate, "but we didn't come here to tell you that. There's something you need to tell all your greasy mates when they arrive later."

Jokerman was staring at Judy as if he didn't quite know who she was. Her hair made her look quite different, but he was sure that he knew her from somewhere.

Nester went on, "You see, Turd, your lot did something a few months ago to our mate's scooter, which has pissed me off ever since. You might recognise Little Pete here, as you threatened him at the time. We've dropped by to tell you that we haven't forgotten. You had better keep your eyes on your fucking greasy bikes, because one day we will get you back."

Turd knew Nester well enough to know that he was not joking. He also knew that, even with girls around, a fight right now would end up badly for him and Jokerman.

"OK, got it. I'll let them know. Now, why don't you all just piss off?" said Turd as aggressively as he dared.

Judy thought that she had got away unnoticed. Suddenly, the door of the Busy Bee Café flew open, and Jimmy was striding out towards them.

"I heard all of that, you prick; if you think that scares us, then you must be fucking mad. Now, as Turd just said, why don't you just piss off while you still can?"

Jimmy was furious. Judy was shocked—she had never seen that side of him before.

At that moment, the penny dropped with Jokerman. He recognised Judy. He turned to stop Jimmy from seeing her, but it was too late. Jimmy recognised her instantly. His heart skipped a beat the same way it had the very first time he saw her at the sweet shop almost two years ago. His expression changed immediately. Terry could see he was looking his way, or rather, Judy's way.

"You heard me. Fuck off while you can."

He didn't want to say anything to Judy. He was just happy that she was back. He would search for her later.

The Mods twisted their grips and accelerated their scooters out of the bike park, shouting and making V-sign gestures as they left. Jokerman turned to Jimmy.

"Did you see that bird on the back of that Terry's scooter? I think it was Judy."

"It was Judy—you are right, mate. Even as a Mod, she looks wonderful. I didn't want to embarrass her, so I didn't say anything."

"You didn't need to say anything, Jimmy," replied Jokerman, "she could see that you recognised her. So did her feller. Your expression gave it away immediately. They were lucky because, if you hadn't seen her, I think that you were ready to kick off and wade into a fight."

"I was, mate. Cheeky little fuckers riding in here as bold as brass. I was ready to get stuck in," he muttered halfheartedly. He was still wondering about Judy.

"Good job you didn't," interrupted Turd. "I grew up with Nester, the one who did the talking. He can really handle himself; I doubt even Jokerman could take him out. And as for Terry whose, real name is Jess; he is smart and every bit as capable. I grew up with him as well. So, with three others to help them out, we would have really struggled."

"No worries. There will be a next time when we will dictate the terms. In the meantime, let's stay silent about Judy. I want to handle that myself without local gossip, please," requested Jimmy.

Jokerman and Turd nodded, and they went back into the Busy Bee Café.

The Mods drew into the Lynx car park and pulled their scooters on to their stands. Terry turned to Judy.

"Do you know those guys? Especially the tall one at the end—he looked straight through me, focusing on you. His expression changed as if he knew you."

Adopting her no secrets and new life attitude, she nodded.

"You didn't give me a chance to speak before we left Radlett. Yes, I know them. Or perhaps I should say that I knew them a long time ago. Jimmy, the one who spoke at the end, and I had a brief fling, but that's all history now."

"For you, maybe, but not for him. He looked straight through me. He almost melted when he saw you," Terry said, concerned that the tall biker still had strong affections for Judy.

"Well, that's his problem, not mine," Judy said firmly as she dismounted the scooter.

 "Are we going to go in and enjoy Georgie Fame or stay out here discussing a pointless encounter that was brought about by your desire to get one back on them?"

She was angry now.

"OK, OK. Keep your hair on."

Terry jumped off his scooter put his arm around her. He whispered in her ear,

"I like it when you get angry. It turns me on."

He kissed her on the cheek and smiled as they went into the Lynx.

Georgie Fame and the Blue Flames were fantastic. Afterwards, they all went their separate ways to drop the girls off then head home. Judy dismounted outside her house.

She kissed Terry, then whispered in his ear, "You are the only one for me."

She smiled, kissed him once more, and disappeared into her house. Terry rode off back towards Elstree, then on to Borehamwood, happy that his girl was still very much his.

As he passed the Duck Pond leaving Letchmore Heath, he didn't notice the dark silhouette of a figure sitting by the road on his bike smoking a cigarette. Jimmy had witnessed Judy entering her home. He vowed to himself that he would get in contact with her in the next few weeks.

As Judy's head hit the pillow, she recognised that she had not been completely truthful with Terry. She knew that Jimmy still had a very special place in heart. She fell asleep completely confused.

Tuesday 23rd March 1965

Terry and Nester had decided to strike whilst the iron was hot. Terry now had a good reason not to like the big Rocker known as Jimmy and agreed with Nester to mount a daring spoof on the bikers as a reprisal for Little Pete's scooter ending up in Aberystwyth. The two of them rode past the Busy Bee to assess the number of bikes parked up. There were just five bikes that evening, so they agreed to execute their plan.

Nester rode back to Radlett and collected a very thick but long chain from his dad's shed. He also picked up a padlock. Terry had stayed close to the Busy Bee to check if more bikers turned up. When Nester returned, Terry confirmed that there were still just five bikes in the bike park. It was 7.30pm and dark enough for them to set their trap.

They left their scooters in Radlett Road and made their way to the Busy Bee on foot. Terry, who was the lookout, positioned himself on the other side of the A41. Nester stooped down and crept to the bike park carrying the thick chain and padlock. He edged his way to the bikes, which were far enough from the café for him not to be seen. He then threaded the chain through the front wheels of all five bikes, padlocking the chain together and covering it as much as possible with all the loose gravel he could find. The chain was thick enough to need an angle grinder to cut through it. Unless they had one behind the bar in the Busy Bee, those bikes weren't going anywhere in a hurry.

They made their way back to their scooters, kick-started them and rode round to the Busy Bee. They roared into the bike park as noisily as they could, sounding their horns and gesticulating to the Rockers inside. The door swung open, and out ran Jimmy, Jokerman, Turd, Grumpy and Madman, shouting, "Right, you fuckers. You've had it now!"

Terry and Nester sped out of the bike park and onto the A41, roaring with laughter. The Rockers jumped on their bikes and, not noticing the chain, kick-started their bikes and tried to make chase. Immediately they collapsed in a heap, scratching their bikes in the process. Jimmy was livid, as his precious new Triumph got scratched quite badly on the petrol tank.

By this time, Terry and Nester had done a U-turn and were cruising back past the Busy Bee, gesticulating with their hands, yelling and yelling, "We're quits now, you wankers!"

They rode off towards Radlett. It took 2 hours to arrange for Bumper to get to the Busy Bee with an angle grinder and a further hour to cut through the chain. Terry and Nester were long gone. They felt very pleased with themselves.

They enjoyed reliving the spoof with the gang. Everyone thought it was very funny. Little Pete was particularly pleased but would have preferred to have been there in person. The girls all thought it was a bit silly and puerile. Judy thought it could only lead to more confrontation, which would not be good for anyone. Terry just shrugged, concluding that it had to be done.

Brighton Riot

Easter Monday 19th April 1965

Shops were closed on Good Friday, Easter Sunday and Easter Monday, so Judy was enjoying some time off work. There was a Mod rally organised for Easter Monday in Brighton. The whole gang decided to go for the ride. It would be a pleasant day out at the seaside.

They met up at Round Bush at 9am. All the girls were there. Everyone was wearing parkas and looking very mod. They set off through the centre of London and out the other side, then headed south towards Crawley and over the South Downs to Brighton. As they left Crawley, it was clear that this was no ordinary rally.

There were literally thousands and thousands of scooters heading towards Brighton.

As they rode through Brighton towards the seafront, the congestion was such that the police were forced to direct the traffic. The police funnelled the scooters onto the promenade to park up. There were over five thousand scooters. The buzz was electric as all the Mods walked on to the beach, singing, chanting and generally being loud, making it uncomfortable for families that had ventured out for a day by the sea. Terry, Judy and the rest of the gang stuck together in the jostling crowd, not sure that this was much fun.

Suddenly, three Rockers were spotted further up the beach.

Someone shouted, "Rockers, let's get them!"

It started a stampede as thousands of Mods took flight to catch and harm the three, now desperate, Rockers. There was no choice. Everyone had to run, or risk being knocked over in the charge. Families took refuge as close to the promenade wall as they could. Children were crying and screaming as this angry mob charged after the three lone Rockers.

Terry, Judy and the others managed to veer off towards the promenade wall. Reaching the wall, they stood with their backs as close to the wall as they could. Watching the stampede continue, the girls were very frightened as they witnessed other female Mods falling onto the stony beach and being trampled on by the charging mob.

Terry and Nester ran across to help one poor girl to her feet and took her back to the wall for safety. Suddenly the mob chasing the Rockers were now being chased by policemen brandishing their truncheons, literally wrestling some of the mob to the ground. It was almost a riot. In fact, it would be described as such in the national newspapers the following day.

One of the Rockers was caught, almost kicked to death and hospitalised. Terry, Judy and the gang escaped unscathed. They made their way to their scooters and left for home as quickly as they could. They all agreed that what was supposed to be a nice day out turned into a disaster. Little did they know that they would experience something even more shocking again that summer, but this time in Margate.

Battle at the Crown Pub

Friday 30th April 1965

Judy was working late, as the supermarket closed at 8pm on Friday evenings. She had agreed with Terry that she would stay home that evening, as she had to work on Saturday morning.

Her dad picked her up from work. She went home for what she thought would be a quiet evening.

Her mum had saved her a dinner, and she sat in the kitchen eating when there was a knock at the front door. She heard her dad shouting at someone on the doorstep.

"Go away! She's moved on with her life and doesn't want to see you."

He went to close the door, but a size ten motorbike boot blocked the way.

By now, Judy was in the hall and staring at Jimmy, who was insisting that he speak to Judy.

"Fuck off. You've caused enough problems for this family—leave us alone!" Judy's dad hollered. He was red in the face and looked like he wanted to physically fight the intruder to his home.

Judy shouted, "Leave it, Dad! I'll see you, Jimmy."

She pushed past her dad, pulled the door closed and walked outside.

"What do you want, Jimmy? You and I are distant history. I've moved on; I'm not the Judy that you knew then."

"I need to talk to you to understand what happened. Where did you disappear to? What caused you to leave? I loved you, Judy. I still do. I need some answers to help me understand why it all came to a stop so suddenly. I deserve that much, at least. Please, Judy. What did your dad mean when he said that I have caused enough problems for your family?" Jimmy pleaded with her.

"You deserve nothing, Jimmy. How dare you turn up here as if you are some kind of victim?" Judy hissed. She felt anger boil up, but she didn't want him to know what had really happened, so she gathered her composure.

"Promise me that you will never turn up at my house again, Jimmy, and I will agree to meet you one more time for a sensible discussion. Promise me, Jimmy."

Judy was firm; he could see that she meant business. Jimmy nodded.

"I promise."

"OK. I have a half-day on Wednesday, 12th May. That's the week after next. If you really want a final chat, I will meet you in the car park at Radlett cricket ground at 2pm. It is quiet there. We can wrap this up once and for all."

She and turned knocked on the door, which was opened immediately, and went inside.

"What did you say to that scumbag?" her dad said. He was still seething. "You've moved on with your life, Judy. You have a nice boyfriend in Terry. You don't need someone like him."

"Dad, I told you when I came back from that hellhole in Ireland, where you and Mum just dumped me to save your own embarrassment, that I would not be told what I can do and what I can't do. I won't be told who I can and can't associate with. I will take responsibility for my own actions from now on. If you don't like it, I will move out and find a flat or room of my own."

Judy was determined to make her point. She was looking as much at her mother as her father when she spoke. They seemed to get the message.

Meanwhile, Terry, Nester and the rest were enjoying a Friday night out at the Crown pub on the corner of Theobald Street and the High Street in Borehamwood. The Zombies, a local band, were playing later that evening. The place was packed, mostly with blokes. It seemed that the whole of Borehamwood was enjoying a boys' night out.

The jukebox was playing a new song by The Rolling Stones called 'Satisfaction'. Everyone was acknowledging the quality of this new single. It was followed by 'The Sun Ain't Gonna Shine (Anymore)' by The Walker Brothers, who were booked to play at the Lynx Club later that month, and then, 'I Got You Babe' by Sonny and Cher. The air was thick with cigarette smoke, the atmosphere seemed a little like a tinderbox—one spark and it might all kick off.

Terry had just been to the bar to get a round in. Everybody was drinking pints of Tartan bitter when in walked Jokerman, Turd, Bumper and Madman. Terry shot them a glance. He noticed that their leader was not with them. Nevertheless, dressed in their leathers, they were clearly out of place in what was essentially a Mod pub. They made a beeline for Terry and Nester, pushing their way towards them.

Pushing people out of the way in the Crown was not a clever thing to do at the best of times, as fights broke out there almost every week for much less than spilling someone's beer in a quest to get at your target. Sure enough, Turd pushed some guy out of the way, spilling most of his beer in the process. That was all it took. The place burst into a fight worthy of any Wild West cowboy saloon punch-up.

Turd was floored by the guy whose beer he had spilt. Jokerman took the guy out with one punch, and others joined in. Madman leapt at a group of four guys, taking two down before he was knocked to the ground himself. Bumper was doing his best to avoid being hit before a beer bottle crashed onto his head.

Cher's voice rang out from the jukebox. "They say your hair's too long, but I don't care. With you, I can't go wrong." Punches were flying everywhere. Then a chair was thrown across the bar, smashing the engraved mirror behind the optics. The barmaid had ducked just in time, avoiding the chair but getting showered by broken glass.

Nester could handle himself in these situations. Between him and Yankee, they waded into battle, trying to stop the fighting. The bar staff were yelling out that the police were on their way. A small table went flying through the air, crashing through a plate glass window out on to the street.

"I got you to hold my hand. I got you to understand. I got you, and I won't let go; I got you to love me, so I got you, babe," rang out Sonny and Cher.

Terry, Shadow and Little Pete did their best to stay out of the fight, but eventually all three were having to defend themselves. Terry turned around and found himself face-to-face with Jokerman.

But before Jokerman could land a punch, he was jumped upon by Nester. They wrestled on the floor, both throwing punches. Terry tried to pull them apart but took a right hook from Jokerman for his troubles.

It looked like a war scene. Tables and chairs were broken. Bodies were lying on the ground. The fighting continued until the sirens were heard. The police ran into the pub. Jokerman and Nester sensed an opportunity to flee before the arrests started being made as the police waded in with truncheons to stop the fighting.

Everyone except Bumper, Shadow and Little Pete got out and legged it up the road to safety. Jokerman turned to Nester.

"We're not done, you and me. There will be a next time."

"You bet your sweet fucking life there will be," replied Nester. "Now, let's fuck off before we all end up in clink for the night."

With that, they ran off in different directions.

The next day, Bumper, Shadow and little Pete were released without charge. The police advised them to stay away, or at least stay out of trouble, as it was only a caution this time. Next time, they would be charged with disturbing the peace or even causing grievous bodily harm, which, if they were found guilty, would mean a prison sentence.

They shuddered at the thought, taking on board the warning.

When Judy heard about the affray, she was furious that the two groups had gotten into a fight. Once her anger had subsided, she then expressed concern at Terry's black eye.

He shrugged it off as if it were nothing, promising to stay out of trouble in the future.

Judy realised that her feelings for Terry were growing ever stronger. Jimmy turning up at her house had sent her to bed very confused, but she was not so confused when she woke the next day. She was in love with Terry, and she was determined to ensure that Jimmy understood that they were finished. She had moved on.

The Links Club - Borehamwood

Saturday 8th May 1965

Terry was waiting outside Bishop's Supermarket in Radlett for Judy to finish work. The plan was for her to stay at his house in Borehamwood. They had tickets to see the Walker Brothers at the Lynx Club. She had only met his mum and dad a few times, finding them down-to-earth, everyday people. She laughed when Terry's dad asked her why she called him Terry when his real name was Jess.

Once Judy had explained their first meeting, he laughed.

"Good on you, girl. That'll teach him. Cocky bugger. You should have asked him if it was short for Theressa, given his hair makes him look like a girl," he laughed loudly.

Judy was shown to the spare room with a single bed, a dressing table and a nice wardrobe. The décor was pink; this was clearly a girl's room. Earlier, Judy had found out that it was Terry's older sister's bedroom. Apparently she had left home out of the blue when she was twenty one, and rarely kept in contact, which left her parents heartbroken.

All they knew was that she was living in Clapham and working in London as an assistant secretary. Young women caught without an education, faced with factory or shop work before hoping to land a husband and settling down to a life of domesticity, often left home in their early twenties to escape.

The attraction of city living became a successful refuge for few. Many fell foul of exploitation, finding that they had escaped only to live a life on the streets.

A broken heart was something Judy could really understand, as she had experienced unimaginable loss when her baby was taken away from her at the Magdalene Laundry. Although she had tried to move on with her life, not a day had passed where she had not thought about her baby girl. She thought that Terry's mum must be going through a similar anguish every single day. She wondered if talking about the loss would help. But she knew that she could not tell anyone about her lost child, especially Terry, who she was beginning to think could be her lifelong partner. Although, apart from the orgasms on the train from the Marquee Club, she had no idea if they would be passionate and sexually compatible.

"Penny for your thoughts?" said Terry, standing in the doorway of her room.

"Oh, nothing really. I was wondering if we might get some privacy tonight, that's all," she replied coolly.

"We can try when we get home, but not upstairs, as my mum is a light sleeper. We can get a bit of time downstairs on the sofa, as they will be in bed by the time we get in," he said with a wink and a smile.

The Lynx was packed that night. The DJ was playing warm-up songs ahead of the live act.

'Stop in the Name of Love' was playing. It was a new record by the Supremes, a three-piece group of Black girls released by the Tamla Motown label. This was the first Black-owned record company in the USA. Tamla Motown was founded in Detroit in 1959 by Berry Gordy, who had met Smokey Robinson, a seventeen-year-old singer fronting a local harmony group called the Matadors. Between Gordy and Robinson, Tamla Motown went on to become the best-known label for soul music, which was known as the Motown sound. Motown sound and its artists were adopted by the Mods in the UK.

The Lynx was rocking to the Supremes when the DJ followed it up with Dusty Springfield singing her latest hit, *In the Middle of Nowhere*, which had just been released. It was destined to reach number four in the charts. Dusty Springfield was thought to be the best white female soul singer in the world. Not many white singers could match the soul sound produced by the Black singers in the US, especially those released by Motown. But Dusty was in a league of her own.

The crowded hall of swinging Mods were now was and truly warmed up when the DJ stopped the music.

"All you Mods out there, put your hands together and welcome to the stage, all the way from America, the Walker Brothers!"

A huge roar went up as John Walker (real name John Maus), Scott Walker (real name Noel Scott Engel) and Gary Walker (real name Gary Leeds) ran onto the stage. Every girl in the hall swooned and gasped as they sang their first song, 'Make It Easy on Yourself'. The deep, sexy voices from these three handsome American hunks captured the hearts of every female in the hall as they swayed back and forth, starry-eyed.

Terry swayed behind Judy, clasping his hands in front of her waist. Pressed close together, they swayed to the sexy sound of the music. Finally, they sang 'The Sun Ain't Gonna Shine (Anymore)', their biggest hit. The whole hall swayed in unison, boys clutching girls, all lost in the moment. For most of them, it was setting the scene for a romantic evening that followed.

After the encore of 'My Ship is Coming In', everyone left just after 11.30pm. No drinking or pills had been involved, just plenty of cigarettes. The fresh night air was welcomed as they rode back to Terry's house on his scooter after a fantastic night with no fights breaking out, just plenty of love.

Terry's mum and dad were in bed when they crept in just before midnight. They tiptoed into the lounge, shut the door and quietly got to the couch. The sexy singing by the Walker Brothers had set them in the mood for some romance.

Terry whispered in Judy's ear, "You know that I love you, babe, don't you? I can't wait for our holiday at the end of the month when we can share a bed. But we can't afford to be caught down here naked tonight, so clothes will need to stay on."

It wasn't the sexiest introduction to the next hour or so, but Judy smiled, nodded and embraced him with a long, passionate kiss.

It wasn't long before the fondling began. The frustration of not being able to rip each other's clothes off in steamy passion led to Terry dropping to his knees in front of the seated Judy. With both hands, he found his way up each leg, past her suspender belt. He gently pulled down her knickers, burying his head in her crotch. His tongue found her clitoris, and the excitement started.

Judy slid slightly forward to enable Terry to work his magic. His tongue was flitting around like the darting tongue of a snake. The pleasure was enormous and was complemented by his right hand around the tops of her thighs eventually slipping into her vagina. She desperately wanted to scream out but managed to curtail her instincts. Her breathing was fast and joyous. Then she reached a crescendo and enjoyed a powerful orgasm. Any doubts that she had about their sexual compatibility were dispersed in that wonderful moment. She could not wait for their holiday.

When Terry emerged after her second orgasm, she slumped back on the couch in ecstasy.

He kissed her gently. She slipped down onto her knees to reciprocate. He stopped her.

"You don't have to. I just loved pleasing you, feeling your response."

"I want to, so just relax," whispered Judy as she unbuckled his belt and unzipped his trousers to release his very stiff penis. She caressed it with her hand at first, then, leaning forward, she started to lick it, then fully suck it, rocking her head up and down. She had never done anything like this before. She found it strangely satisfying after the joy of her orgasms.

It didn't take long before Terry tapped her head, as he was breathing heavily and on the verge of coming. But she didn't pull back; she was putting her heart and soul into it as an expression of love.

She felt no shame, just joy as she continued through the throbbing and ejaculation. The taste was strangely good. She swallowed and carried on, ensuring maximum satisfaction for them both.

When she lifted her head and sat down beside Terry, they smiled and kissed a long, sensual kiss, cementing their feelings for each other. At that moment, Judy knew that they were compatible. She recognised that she loved him very much.

Suddenly, Terry's dad's voice rang out.

"Is that you, Jess? Everything OK?"

They rapidly straightened their clothes in case his dad appeared at the door.

"Yes, Dad, we are OK. We're going to bed now."

"OK, good. It's late. See you in the morning!"

His dad had stayed at the top of the stairs, not wishing to find them in a compromising position. He had been young once and could still remember the joys of courting.

They spent the following day with his mum and dad like a newly married couple on a Sunday. They took a trip to the pub, returning to a Sunday roast before Terry took Judy home after a lovely weekend. They weren't due to see each other until the following Friday, as they both had a busy working week ahead of them.

Last Meeting No means No

Wednesday 12th May 1965

Judy made her way to work. It was a bright, sunny spring morning, so she decided to walk the 2 miles to the Bishop's Supermarket. She liked to get there by 7.30am to give herself sufficient time to get her delicatessen counter laid out before opening at 8.30am.

As she made her way up Common Lane towards Radlett, her mind wandered to the meeting that she had arranged for 2pm with Jimmy at Radlett Cricket Ground at the top of Cobden Hill. She was anxious because she really had moved on with her life. She needed to ensure that Jimmy understood that and left her alone for good. She had taken his ring from her drawer and was determined to give it back.

As she was walking down Loom Lane, she heard the familiar sound of a scooter coming up the hill towards her. It was Nester. The scooter came to a stop alongside her.

"Want a lift to work, Judy?" asked Nester.

"No, I'm fine, thanks, Nester. I'm enjoying the walk. What are you doing coming up this way?" she asked inquisitively.

"Oh, I just dropped Jackie off at work and decided to take the country roads to go to work, that's all," came the reply.

"Well, have a good day. Might see you at the weekend," responded Judy.

Nester nodded, selected first gear and sped noisily up the lane. Judy gasped a little as she realised how easy it was to be seen in the village by people that she knew.

She had selected the Cricket Club car park to meet Jimmy at 2pm because it was secluded. Most, if not all, dog walkers would have finished walking their dogs by lunchtime.

The morning passed very slowly. She tried to concentrate, but her mind kept drifting to the meeting she was to have with Jimmy.

Over and over, she rehearsed how she was going to control the discussion, ensuring that he understood that they were over.

The supermarket closed at 1pm. Wednesday was a half day midweek, as all the shop workers had to work all day every Saturday. Judy finished clearing up and cleaning her counter and managed to get away by 1.30pm. As she left, the sun was shining. It was a warm spring day.

It took her 15 minutes to walk to the Cricket Club at the top of Cobden Hill. To her surprise, as she rounded the corner on the entry road to the club, she could see Jimmy waiting for her on his bike. He was smoking a cigarette, blowing the smoke high into the air. He looked every bit as wonderful as he did the day she met him at Mr Stephens' corner shop almost two years ago.

She shook her head, trying to bury any memory of the feelings that she once had for this biker. When she got close, he took one last drag on his cigarette, flicked the butt away and got off his bike.

"Thanks for coming. I was wondering if you would. I am so glad you did," said Jimmy as he walked towards her with outstretched arms.

"I said I would come. I am always true to my word. But Jimmy, this is a discussion. Nothing else."

Judy was stern in her response, and Jimmy nodded sheepishly.

They both turned and walked through the car park to a stile which led to a field. Jimmy hopped over, then held out his hand to help Judy over. She shook her head, determined to keep her distance, as she didn't trust herself not to fall for him all over again.

As she climbed over the stile, her foot caught the top of it and she almost fell. Jimmy was there in a flash and caught her in his arms. She was staring up at the wonderful face that she adored so much all those months ago.

"Careful. I've got you," he murmured.

With that, their eyes met. She felt herself melting.

He moved forward to kiss her, but she ducked away.

"No, Jimmy. We are here to talk," she said, trying to push him back. Jimmy held her tightly; she shook her head in protest, but it was in vain as he kissed her passionately. Her resistance was strong at first, but then it dissolved. She kissed him back, rolling back the months.

They fell to the ground, sheltered from view by a hedge. The passionate embrace continued. With the sun on his back, Judy was powerless to resist his advances. Within minutes they were clawing at each other's clothes, breathing very heavily.

Judy came to her senses; she shook her head and cried, "No, Jimmy, please don't!"

It was too late. She felt Jimmy enter her smoothly, and the passionate embrace was over in a trice. Judy felt sick at that moment.

Jimmy flopped sideways, whispering, "Wow. You are still wonderful."

Judy was crying. Everything that she had planned had gone out of the window. She had succumbed to his advances and was immediately regretting what had just happened.
She sat up and wiped the tears from her eyes. She looked at him sternly.

"I said no, Jimmy! And no means no!

I came here to talk, and look at what just happened! I didn't *want* that to happen. Did you even think to use some protection? You were just thinking of yourself, with no consideration for my feelings. I'm very angry, Jimmy."

"You didn't try hard to push me away. In fact, I felt your resistance subside and thought that you were wrapped up in the moment. I worship the ground you walk on, Judy; I wouldn't do anything to hurt you. No, I didn't use a johnny. It all happened so quickly.

I'm sorry."

She looked at him, furious.

"You're sorry. Is that all you can say? It's me that must deal with any consequences from what we—no, what *you*—just did. That's it, Jimmy. The meeting is over. I'm in love with someone else. I came here to tell you to leave me and my family alone."

She got to her feet, shook her head, straightened her clothes and pointed her finger at him.

"We are through, Jimmy. We were through when I left over a year ago. It's finished; I'm done."

She took his ring from her pocket and threw it at him. She climbed the stile and ran off, cutting through some paths that took her eventually to Common Lane and back home.

Jimmy sat there in tears. He didn't know what had come over him—it was just raw passion for the girl that he thought—no, he knew—that he loved. He was desperately sorry for what had just happened. It took him over an hour to gather his composure, get back to his bike and ride home to Bushey Oxhey, feeling very ashamed.

When Judy got home, she rushed upstairs to the bathroom, ran a hot bath and scrubbed herself almost raw in an effort to wash away the feeling of intrusion that she felt. Why did I not fight harder? What about Terry? I've betrayed him. What if I am pregnant? Oh, God, what a mess. She scrubbed herself as clean as she could.

She told her mum that she was feeling unwell and went to bed early. She sobbed herself to sleep.

When she woke for work the next day, she looked in the mirror. She had not taken her eye makeup off the night before, and her mascara had run in tears down her cheeks. She stared hard in disbelief at the all-too-familiar image staring back at her.

She loved Terry very much. She vowed that she would do everything she could to wipe the incident with Jimmy from her memory. She gave herself a determined look, nodded and mouthed, "I just hope I am not pregnant."

Maddisons Holiday Camp

Saturday 22nd May 1965

Terry and Nester had decided that it would be good to have transport whilst they were away on holiday at Littlestone-on-Sea. They decided to skip the train journey and take the scooters. This meant one small suitcase between each couple strapped to their backrest racks, plus what they would wear on the journey. Their logic was that, since Maddisons Holiday Camp was not in Monaco, it was not a fashion week. They would spend most of their time in swimsuits or, as the boys hoped, in bed. Thus, a small suitcase would be sufficient.

Judy was so looking forward to getting away with Terry that she was up early, dressed and waiting for him to pick her up at 8am. She had packed her clothes the day before. Terry had everything—makeup, toiletries and the essential johnnies in the case strapped to his back rest rack. She had her best smart mod clothes on and her all-important parka ready for his arrival.

She heard him decelerate as he came down the hill into Letchmore Heath, the familiar sound of his two-stroke 200 cc engine popping from his big-bore exhaust. By the time he arrived, she was waiting on the doorstep.

"Morning, gorgeous. Are you ready to be swept away for a romantic week in sunny Kent?" he quipped with a cheeky grin.

He then realised that her parents were standing behind her in the hall, "Oh, sorry, Jack and Mary. I didn't see you there."

"Don't worry, Terry. We hope that you and Danny enjoy sharing a room. Judy will get on OK in her room with Jackie," said Jack with a smile, thinking that at least he had expressed his condition when he agreed to Terry taking Judy away.

"Of course, Jack. I've got my earplugs in case Nest... I mean, Danny snores too much," he responded a little nervously but managed a smile, even though they all knew that he was lying through his teeth.

"Hop on, Judy. It's a long ride, we are meeting the others in Radlett at a quarter past eight."

"Bye, Mum, bye, Dad. See you next weekend! Don't worry; Terry is a safe rider."

They both waved and rode off to meet Nester and Jackie in Radlett.

When they pulled up at the layby outside the post office in Radlett, Nester and Jackie had already arrived.

"Morning, you two. Ready for a long ride? We'll be going through the east end of London, Blackwall Tunnel, the A2, the A27 through Rye and then on to Littlestone-on-Sea, OK?" said Nester.

"Yeah, let's go," smiled Terry, and they set off on their journey.

It was an uneventful journey. The traffic was light for a Saturday morning, so they reached the Blackwall Tunnel in 45 minutes. As they went under the Thames, their big-bore exhausts made a deafening din as they accelerated out the other side onto the A2.

Fifteen miles on, they went right onto the A27, then rode all the way down to Rye. There, they picked up the coast road heading west towards Hastings. Next stop, Littlestone-on-Sea.

The Maddisons Holiday Camp was small in comparison to a Butlins or Pontins Holiday Camp. It had an arched sign supported by two pillars at the entrance reading 'Welcome to Maddisons Holiday Camp'. They rode in, found reception and booked in; luckily, their chalets were next to each other.

"Chalet A26 for Miss Jackie Owens and Miss Judy McDermot and Chalet A27 for Mr Jess King and Mr Danny Ottway," said the receptionist, checking proof of identification and handing the A26 key to Jackie and the A27 to Terry, who she knew as Jess from his driving licence. As she handed over the keys, she gave a knowing look to all four of them, which intimated that she knew that they would end up as couples in the chalets.

"Breakfast starts at 9am and finishes at 10am. You will hear that announced on the Tannoy every morning followed by the 'William Tell Overture'; that's the clue for all the campers to rush to breakfast.

Lunch is between 12.30 and 2pm, and dinner is between 6pm and 7pm. Every evening, there is live music in the ballroom, plus other activities. A full schedule is on this event programme."

"Hm," Terry said, scanning the programme.

"Look here," the receptionist noted, "There's a fancy dress evening, an odd couples evening—that's when the man dresses as a woman and the woman dresses as a man—a dance competition evening and a musical chairs evening.

During the day, there are all sorts of sports activities on the field and in the pool, plus a knobbly knee competition for the men and a Miss Maddisons Beauty competition for the women. It's all listed here. We hope you enjoy your stay with us at Maddisons."

The receptionist finished her spiel with a blush, as she had clearly taken a shine to Nester, much to Jackie's annoyance.

They were able to ride their scooters right up to their chalets and park outside. Jackie and Nester took A26, and Terry and Judy went into A27. It was two in the afternoon.

"See you at 6pm, Nester. We'll be outside and ready to go to the bar before dinner," called out Terry as he and Judy bundled themselves into their chalet with their suitcase.

Terry kicked the door shut as he was almost pulled onto one of the two single beds inside by Judy, who was clawing at his clothes and kissing him passionately.

The room was sparsely furnished with a dressing table, two single beds and a wardrobe. The toilet and shower blocks were about one hundred yards from their chalet. The walls were paper-thin, and any noises would carry outside, letting everyone know what was going on inside.

Neither Judy nor Terry cared. This was the first time that they had been in a private room with nobody to disturb them since they had first met. They were giggling, kissing and pulling each other's clothes off at the same time.

"I love you, Judy," whispered Terry.

"I love you too, very much," was the reply.

Within seconds, they were working each other up into a frenzy as if all the frustration that had built up since they had first met was let out in that very moment.

They were both ready to cement their relationship. They made passionate love to each other. Terry slipped inside, caressing Judy with a tenderness and respect that she had come to expect from him. She caressed him back, filled with love and affection.

Suddenly, just as they were reaching a crescendo, Terry stopped, whispering, "I need to put on a johnny."

But they were too close. Judy held him tightly, manoeuvring her hips to rock with his; they were truly making love. Terry came at the same time as Judy. They both let out a pleasurable groan. They flopped back on to the bed, side by side, and smiled.

Terry looked at her and said, "Judy McDermott, I love you, but we must be more careful this week. I have brought enough johnnies for us to never leave the bedroom for six days. We should use them to be safe."

Judy looked into Terry's eyes and nodded. Then she added, "My period is due in about twelve days. We should be fine this far away for just one time. Thank you for being so considerate. We must use a johnny from now on and not take any risks. Now, where are they? Shall we do that again?" she teased. But, in the back of her mind, she had just secured an insurance policy in case she was pregnant from the incident with Jimmy earlier in the month.

And they did indeed do it again and again and again before getting unpacked and ready for dinner.

As they left their chalet, Nester, who was sitting outside on his scooter smoking a fag waiting for Jackie to finish putting on her makeup, said, "Blimey. You two have been at it all afternoon! You must be knackered."

"And you haven't, I suppose? Maybe you have both been reading a book or sleeping, but judging by the noises coming from your chalet, we are one or two behind you and Jackie—that's for sure," laughed Terry.

"What are you two boasting about? It's not a competition, you know," growled Jackie as she locked the chalet to go to dinner, "because if it was, we would win."

She laughed and grabbed Nester's hand, and the four of them sauntered off to the bar for a pre-dinner drink.

The food was bearable. They laughed and enjoyed the evening; the holiday had well and truly started. They decided to hit the sack early after a long journey and the exertions of the afternoon.

The week at Maddisons Holiday Camp Littlestone-on-Sea

The week at Maddisons Holiday Camp at Littlestone-on-Sea was one that none of them would ever forget—a perfect blend of carefree pleasure, youthful passion and light-hearted fun. The holiday camp buzzed with life, a vibrant oasis of pastel-coloured chalets neatly lined in rows, each with a small porch and cheerful curtains fluttering in the sea breeze. Laughter and the distant sound of a brass band spilled from the central entertainment hall, where the guests gathered for afternoon tea and the evening cabaret. The air smelled of salt and vinegar from the fish and chip stand, mingling with the sweet scent of candyfloss from the amusement arcade.

Judy and Terry woke at around 8 am on the first morning. Like all young couples deeply in love and tasting true freedom for the first time, they immediately embraced each other with fervent passion. Their connection, which had blossomed the night before over dinner, only deepened as they explored each other's desires. They had started to understand what each other liked. That morning, Judy confidently slipped a Johnny onto Terry's erect penis, then straddled him with a playful smile as he lay on his back. They both enjoyed that position, each reaching a climax twice before Judy rolled off at two minutes to nine in the morning, before the loud Tannoy burst into life.

As the unmistakable notes of the 'William Tell Overture' blared from the loudspeaker. They both jumped, startled. Laughter soon replaced their surprise as they heard the thunder of feet outside.

Campers stampeded across the playing field from their chalets, racing toward the restaurant for breakfast. Sharing a fag, Judy and Terry glanced at each other and broke out into a fit of laughter. The week was off to a fabulous start.

The quartet—Terry, Judy, Nester and Jackie—were determined to make the most of their week and throw themselves into the camp's lively atmosphere. They signed up for every competition they could. Nester's suggestion that they make love each morning to the 'William Tell Overture' became an inside joke that left them giggling uncontrollably. The camp itself was mostly filled with older couples—ancient in their eyes at over forty! Thankfully, because it was term time, there were few children about, which everyone agreed was a blessing.

The competitions were a riot of laughter and fun. Terry and Nester entered the Knobbly Knee contest, only to be beaten by much older, more knobbly-legged competitors. They both agreed that their legs were far too sexy for such a contest. Judy and Jackie entered the beauty competition and were delighted when Judy was crowned Miss Maddisons and Jackie the runner-up.

The ballroom dancing competition was perhaps the most hilarious event. Though Judy and Jackie knew the basic steps of the waltz and foxtrot, Terry and Nester were utterly hopeless on the dance floor, with their two left feet a constant hindrance. During the quickstep, Terry's legs tangled disastrously, sending him crashing to the floor with Judy nearly falling on top of him. Everyone watching roared with laughter.

The odd couple competition was even better. Terry dressed as a woman, with Judy as a man. Judy's short, cropped hair worked perfectly with a mascara-drawn moustache, transforming her into a dashing figure.

Terry, meanwhile, looked surprisingly convincing as a woman. Judy's skilful hairdressing and careful makeup application made him look almost attractive. When Judy snapped a photo, she found that she couldn't wait to show it to Terry's dad, imagining the look on his face.

"Blimey, mate," Nester joked, "I almost fancy you myself—but only almost!"

The group dissolved into laughter again.

When the two of them stepped onto the dance floor, the audience clapped and cheered. There was no doubt who would win the contest, and they did—by a mile. Later that night, the couple couldn't stop giggling as they made love, still half in their odd-couple costumes—Judy with her moustache and Terry with his makeup. They were having the time of their lives.

The week flew by in a whirlwind of sunny days and secret moments. They nearly ran out of johnnies, sneaking off to their chalet whenever they found a quiet moment. The weather stayed beautiful, allowing for long sunbathing sessions around the pool. Suntan oil became their playful excuse for impromptu massages that always ended with a dash back to their chalet to continue what had begun in private.

Before they knew it, it was time to leave. They packed their things with reluctance, savouring every last moment. As they checked out, the sun shone down on them. The receptionist gave Nester a cheeky wink, prompting a glare from Jackie.

"Come again soon," she said with a grin.

The ride back was easy, and they arrived mid-afternoon on Saturday, 29th May 1965.

Terry dropped Judy off, and they agreed to have a rest day on Sunday because Monday 31st was a bank holiday. They were going to Margate for a Mod festival. Terry arranged to pick Judy up at 8am on Monday.

Judy had enjoyed telling her parents all about the week at the holiday camp. They laughed when she told them how Terry had tripped doing the quickstep and how easily they had looked an odd couple, with Terry being very convincing as a woman, winning first prize. But Jack and Mary McDermott were most proud when she showed them her picture as Miss Maddisons, with Jackie as the runner-up and another girl in third place.

"Fancy that. Our girl as a beauty queen after all that has happened," said Jack, puffing out his chest.

Judy frowned a little, given that he had dumped her in Ireland just to save face in Letchmore Heath and now was crowing with pride.

Margate The Final Reckoning

Sunday 30th May 1965

Judy woke early to the smell of fried bacon wafting up from the kitchen. At first, she lay there looking back on the week with a big grin on her face, but then a sudden wave of nausea swept through her body. She knew that feeling well. Making as little noise as possible, she made her way to the loo, where she was sick, flushing the toilet to camouflage the sound of her vomiting.

Her control over her body this time was much better. She was convinced that neither her mum nor dad would have heard her above the noise from the radio and the sizzling of the bacon downstairs. Back in her room, she stared at her reflection in the mirror in disbelief.

She knew in her heart that it was probably too soon for this pregnancy, if indeed she was pregnant, to be because of the holiday camp sex. She feared the worst, that most likely it was because of the horrible encounter with Jimmy ten days ago.

If she was pregnant, she knew exactly what she wanted to do this time. She would keep it a secret from her parents, ensuring that she controlled her sickness so that neither of them heard her vomiting. She would get a test in a week or so. If it was positive, she would only tell Terry in the hope that he would ask her to marry him. They could live together, renting a flat somewhere. Yes, she thought, that's it. She was determined to turn this situation into a positive outcome for herself, Terry and her unborn baby.

Monday 31st May 1965

Terry arrived early that morning and was having bacon and eggs with her mum and dad when Judy came downstairs at 7.30am.

"Blimey, you're early," she said, fighting back the urge to be sick at the sight and smell of the fried breakfast.

"Your mum encouraged me to come for breakfast when I dropped you off on Saturday. We were just laughing about the holiday and the stories you told them," said Terry with a big grin.

"Eggs and bacon, love?" asked Judy's mum.

"No thanks, Mum. Just tea and toast for me, please," came the reply.

"Come on, love. It's a long ride to Margate and you'll need more than that to set you up for the day," said Judy's dad.

"No, really. Two bits of toast and some tea will be fine, thanks."

Judy was assertive now, although she had no idea if she could quell the nausea that she could feel bubbling up in her stomach.

"OK, there you go. Tea and toast. Now, sit down and tell us some more about your holiday last week," prompted Judy's mum.

They chatted away, Judy managing to keep her tea and toast down. She reflected on the happy family atmosphere that the four of them were sharing in contrast to the way things felt the last time she felt this sick each morning. It made her even more determined to manage her own destiny this time.

They set off at 8am and met the rest of the gang in Radlett, who were waiting in the layby outside the post office. The whole gang was ready: Nester and Jackie, Yankee and Julie, Shadow and Gill, Little Pete and Carol... Terry pulled in and nodded to them all.

"Thought we would go out east to the Dartford Tunnel, then onto the M2, then Thanet Way and then Margate. What do you think?' Terry asked Nester.

"Fine by me" came the reply, and the rest nodded.

The five scooters headed off towards Barnet, making a hell of a racket as they left Radlett.

It was a lovely sunny day with not a cloud in the sky. They made good time—they exited the Dartford Tunnel, and when they turned on to the A2/M2, they joined a procession of scooters streaming out of

London. By the time they reached the halfway café on the M2 to stop for a loo break, petrol and a cuppa, the two-lane motorway was packed with scooters heading towards the coast.

"Bloody hell, have you ever seen so many scooters before? There are even more than when we went to Brighton," commented Nester.

"Let's hope it's a fun day and not like Brighton. I'm here to enjoy myself—not to have any fights," said Terry. The others nodded in agreement.

Meanwhile, back in Letchmore Heath, Mary McDermott had cleared away the breakfast things and was waiting for Jack to come downstairs to go out for the day to Whipsnade Zoo when there was a knock at the door.

She answered the door and gasped.

Jimmy had his foot in the door and was demanding, "Where is she? Where's Judy? I must see her right now."

He was almost inside the house when Jack came running down the stairs, shouting, "Get out, you bastard! How dare you come crashing into my house like this?"

Jack was red in the face and grabbed Jimmy by the neck.

"Calm down, Mr McDermott," cried Jimmy as he easily shoved Jack to the ground. Jack realised the strength gap was too great between himself and this unwelcome biker. He thought better of fighting back.

"Where is she?" Jimmy shouted again.

"She's not here. She's gone out for the whole day to Margate, so please leave us alone," begged Mary, now in tears.

"What did you mean, Mr McDermott, when you said I caused your family enough trouble last time we met? Come on, tell me. What did you *mean*?"

Jimmy was emotional and getting very agitated. Jack became concerned about what he might do to them.

Jack hit back, "You, you bastard, very nearly destroyed my family. If we had not sent Judy away for a while, it would have been over for us!"

"But what do you *mean*? I did nothing but love your daughter! How is that destroying your family?" Jimmy sobbed. He was shaking now, tears flooding down his face.

"You got her pregnant," Jack spat.

There was a deafening silence. Jimmy looked at him, wide-eyed.

"That's what you did, you bastard," Jack continued through gritted teeth. "Now, piss off and leave us alone from now on, or I will go to the police. You are harassing this family."

Jack McDermott stopped, realising what he had done in revealing to Jimmy that Judy had been pregnant.

Jimmy gasped, shook and held his head in his hands.

"The Johnny that split," he whispered to himself.

"What's that? What did you say? Speak up, you bastard," yelled Jack.

"Nothing. I said nothing. I must find her. Margate, did you say? I'll catch them up."

With that, Jimmy left in a hurry. He jumped on his bike and shot off, heading east to the Dartford Tunnel.

At that moment, Jokerman, Turd, Madman and Bumper roared into Letchmore Heath looking for Jimmy.

Mary went to close the door when Jokerman shouted at her, "Wait! Please wait. What's happened? Has Jimmy been here looking for Judy?"

Jack came to the door.

"Yes, he came here terrorising this family. Now, to make things worse, he is storming off to Margate to find Judy, who is trying to enjoy a day out with her boyfriend. The guy is completely mad."

"Bloody hell!" yelled Jokerman. "Come on, guys. We must try and catch him up. Leave your bike here, Turd. Jump on with Madman—it will be quicker that way."

Turd left his bike outside the McDermott's cottage, and they all sped off to chase down Jimmy, hoping to stop him from getting into trouble or, worse still, doing something stupid.

As Terry, Nester and the others left the M2 and joined the Thanet Way, passing Whitstable with fifteen miles to go to Margate, the scooters were four abreast on a three-lane road where the middle lane was an overtaking lane. They were nose to tail. There must have been over ten thousand scooters streaming towards Margate.

As they drew into Margate, the police, who were well prepared this time, were marshalling the scooters to the front so that they could park up by the beach where the police could keep an eye on them. Terry and the gang parked up opposite Margate Dreamland, a theme park complete with a roller coaster and big wheel. It was almost noon, so they decided to get a Wimpy burger, chips and a milkshake before heading into Dreamland for some fun.

The sea front was buzzing, with amusement arcades, candyfloss, 'Kiss Me Quick' hats and flashing light bulbs everywhere. There was a general sense that summer was just around the corner.

Margate was the place to be in 1965. Music bellowed out from everywhere. You could hear the Who's 'My Generation' coming out of one arcade. The Mods had arrived. They were taking over Margate on that bank holiday Monday.

Once they had eaten their burgers and chips, they headed for Dreamland, thinking that it was safer in there than on the beach. First, they headed for the Big Dipper. They took up the first five lots of two seats. Nester took off his pork pie hat to save losing it on the ride. The train locked on to the chain, and they were dragged clunk by clunk up to the top of the Big Dipper's wooden structure. Terry and Judy were at the front. As the train of carriages reached the top, there was a moment's pause. Suddenly, they zoomed down the other side. The girls screamed loudly. The wooden structure seemed to creak and groan as the train raced around the bends, up and down the ride.

It was an exhilarating experience.

Next stop, the big wheel. The sky was free of clouds, the sea was calm and the tide was in the bay. People were swimming in the sea.

The beach was full of Mods wandering up and down. As they rode on the big wheel, it stopped to let people off and others on. Terry, Judy, Nester and Jackie were right at the top, so they could see the whole of Margate Bay beneath them.

Suddenly, Judy screamed, "Look, Terry! Look down there! Is that Jimmy being chased by those Mods? And look over there—that's Jokerman and the others running after Jimmy!"

"Fucking hell—you're right! Nester, we need to get off this thing and help those guys. It's alright for us to fight with them, but they are from our manor, and we can't just let this happen," yelled Terry.

Nester nodded and shouted down to the big wheel operator, "Hey, mate! We need to get off this thing, fast!"

The operator nodded up to them and set the wheel moving, bringing it to a halt to let them all off.

Terry shouted to Judy to wait at the front of Dreamland with the other girls. He, Nester and the other guys ran out across the road, down onto the beach and into the affray.

Judy was not going to wait anywhere. Together with Jackie, she crossed over to get to the beach. Jimmy was running towards them and shouting something. Jokerman and the other rockers were about twenty yards behind. Terry, Nester and the other guys were running towards Jimmy with thirty yards to go.

Fifty or more Mods came running in from the left, shouting loudly, "Get the bastard! Let him have it!"

They got to Jimmy first, who was shouting Judy's name.

They jumped on Jimmy. He fell to the ground, fighting as he went down. These were South London Mods who had come prepared for a fight. One of them pulled out a knife as they all waded in, kicking and hitting Jimmy as he lay sprawled on the ground. The one with the knife thrust it forward, stabbing Jimmy just below his heart. Blood sprayed out. All the Mods jumped back, staring at Jimmy on the sand.

At that moment, Jokerman ran in screaming, yelling and throwing punches everywhere. Almost instantly the mob backed up and fled, leaving Jimmy lying on the blood-soaked sand. Jokerman ran to his mate and cradled his head. He screamed, "Someone get help! A doctor or an ambulance—anything! Get someone!"

Terry, Nester and the others ran in, stopping abruptly when they saw Jimmy lying lifeless. Jokerman was sobbing, still holding his friend. Terry turned and saw Judy running in. He tried to stop her, but she slipped through.

She went to bend down, but Terry took her arm.

"It's too late, Judy. He's gone."

Jimmy's eyes were staring forward. He had taken his last breath before he could say anything.

Jokerman looked up, tears streaming down his face.

He shouted at them, "Go! Go! Get out! Leave us—it's too late! The police will be here shortly. Just go *away*!"

Turd grabbed Nester.

"Get them out of here, mate," he said, trying to control his shaking. "There's nothing they can do. Go, leave. We can meet up at the Busy Bee later in the week. Now go."

Nester nodded and signalled to the others.

Terry, cuddling Judy, left with Nester and the others. They made their way up the beach and back to the scooters.

Judy was too numb to cry. She was in shock. Jimmy had died in front of her very eyes. The man she had once loved. The man who was the father to a child that he, nor she, ever knew. But she could not mention any of that now. Terry did his best to comfort her.

They all thought it best to leave Margate as quickly as possible. They got on their scooters, heading homewards in complete silence.

They pulled into the halfway café on the M2 for fuel and a break. Judy was white with fear. Grief was etched all over her face.

Terry got her some tea with lots of sugar. They sat together, separate from the others, who were discussing the events that they had just witnessed.

"Get that hot tea down you. It will do you good," murmured Terry as soothingly as he could.

"How did he know we were in Margate?" asked Judy, trembling. "What was he doing there?"

"All good questions, honey, but you won't get any answers here. We have a long way to ride yet. I need to know that you are OK after what has just happened."

Terry had his arm around her. His face was pale with genuine concern.

"OK?" she rounded on him, blinking in disbelief. "What do you mean, OK? I've just watched the guy that I once deeply cared for die in front of my eyes. And you ask me if I'm OK?"

Judy was not angry with Terry, but she was sobbing uncontrollably now.

"Honey, I didn't ask if you are OK with what you just saw. Of course you're not. I meant to ask if you are going to be able to manage the ride home. You're shaking, and I'm just worried. You are all I care about."

Terry was doing his best to console her. He needed, more than anything, to get her home.

Judy stopped sobbing.

"Terry, don't worry about me. We can leave in just a moment. But I need to tell you some things first."

She told Terry how Jimmy had almost burst into her home before their trip to the holiday camp, demanding a meeting.

"I told him that we were finished and that, to save more embarrassment, I would meet him just before our holiday on my half day off," she said.

"We met and talked. I told him that we were through. That I was in love with you. I gave him back his ring. I told him to leave me and my family alone. I have no idea why he turned up today. Believe me, Terry, I told him straight."

Judy had missed out on telling him the gory details of what she considered to be non-consensual sex, as that surely would not help now or anytime in the future.

"Don't worry, love. Let's get you home safely. We can try to understand why he was in Margate later. Come on, you lot. Let's go," Terry said and nodded to the others.

As they approached Radlett, there was lots of waving as they all went their separate ways. Terry turned up Loom Lane, onto Common Lane then down the hill to Letchmore Heath.

As they arrived, the weather changed. It started to rain. Judy knocked on the door, but nobody was home. She could not see her father's car. She assumed that they were still out for the day.

It was now almost six pm. She had a key. She turned slowly to Terry.

"It's trying to rain, so you get home before it does. I will be fine; I think I'll take a bath. I'll call you from the phone box later, once my mum and dad are home." She leaned forward, kissed him gently and smiled, "I'm fine, really. Now, get home before you get soaked."

Terry nodded and set off back towards Borehamwood.

Judy was running a bath when she heard a key in the front door. Her parents were home. She turned off the taps, ran downstairs sobbing and hugged her mum.

"Oh Mum, we have had the most shocking day ever—I can't tell you..."

Her dad cut in.

"Caught up with you, did he? Stupid bastard. He was here not long after you left.

Threatening us—no, harassing us. That's what it was: harassment. I was worried that he was going to attack us."

Judy pulled away from her mum. Anger was rising through her body. She stared fiercely at her dad.

"What did you say to him, Dad? Tell me! *Tell me!*" She shouted—almost screamed—at him, "Come on, Dad. What did you *say* to him?"

Jack McDermott had never seen his daughter look at him that way before. Her cold-hearted stare made him think that something terrible must have happened.

"Now, look here," he said sternly, "your mother and I had no choice but to tell him where you had gone. He was threatening us—he even pushed me to the floor. We were in fear for our safety."

"Is that all you told him, Dad? Because he found us, and now he's *dead*." She was screaming at her father, tears streaming down her cheeks, "He wouldn't have come that way for nothing—not when he could have waited outside the house. Come on, Dad. What else did you *tell* him?"

"Dead? How the hell did that happen? Crashed on that bloody bike, I'd wager," he said. He looked to the ground sheepishly, then looked up. "Nothing, Judy. We told him nothing."

Her mum cut in, "No more lies, Jack. Your dad was under real pressure, love. He told Jimmy that you left because you were pregnant."

The shock pierced Judy like an arrow through her heart. She was furious.

"Dad, you are *incredible*. First, you sent me away because you were embarrassed that your daughter was pregnant. You made me promise never to mention it to anyone, but when you felt threatened, you told the father of my child—the father of your granddaughter—the truth, just to save your own skin. And now he's dead! Well, make bloody sure that you never tell anybody else, because it is my life that needs protecting, not yours anymore."

"Judy—" he stammered.

"Unbelievable," she hissed. "That's it. I'm finished here. I'm leaving. I'll stay at Terry's until I or we can find a flat together. I'm done with you two."

She grabbed her purse and keys, ran out of the cottage and headed to the phone box. The rain was flooding down. She was soaked through to the skin by the time she reached the phone box.

She dialled Terry's house, and his mum answered.

"Can I speak to Terry, please?" she asked, trying to sound calm.

Terry came to the phone.

"You OK, honey? Are your mum and dad home now?"

"Terry, it's awful. My dad told Jimmy where we were, and if he had not done that, Jimmy would still be alive," she blurted. She was crying now. "I'm not staying there a moment longer. I'm leaving home. Can I stay with you for a few days until I find a place to live? Please, Terry, just a few days."

"Of course you can. I can come and get you tomorrow after work."

"No, Terry, I mean tonight. I need to leave right now. Can you borrow your dad's car? Come and get me, please, Terry. I'm begging you."

"OK, I'm on my way. Get your bag packed, and I'll be there in half an hour."

"Thanks. I love you, Terry. Very much." Judy said sincerely.

She hung up and ran back to her house to pack.

She was soaked through. She let herself in, ran upstairs and packed a bag. When she came downstairs, her dad blocked her path.

"And where do you think you are going, young lady?"

"Oh, go *away*, Dad. You know where I'm going. I'm leaving for good. I'll take care of myself from now on. Neither of you should worry about me anymore."

She saw the headlights from the car as Terry pulled up outside.

Judy took a deep breath and pushed past her dad. She opened the door, and without looking back, shouted, "Your keys are upstairs. I'll collect anything I've left behind at some time in the future."

With that, she slammed the front door, got into the car and kissed Terry. They drove away.

Terry's parents were pleased to see Judy, especially after the ordeal she had witnessed in Margate. They agreed that she could stay until something more permanent could be worked out, although later they would try to encourage her to make peace with her parents.

They had experienced the pain of being separated from their daughter for a long time. It was a feeling that they would not wish upon anyone.

Moving On

Tuesday 1st June 1965

It was a bright sunny morning. Judy got ready to face the day, still confused and dazed about the events of the previous day. How could her dad have told Jimmy about her pregnancy? They had agreed, even sworn, to secrecy to avoid any further involvement in the situation. Not to mention the embarrassment that her parents were so desperate to avoid in a small intimate village like Letchmore Heath. She put on a brave face, Terry's mum was very kind, offering breakfast before preparing anything, thankfully avoiding cooking smells that might bring on her nausea.

After tea and toast, Terry gave Judy a lift to work, as his journey to work passed through Radlett on his way to Handley Pages in Park Street. Judy leaned back on the scooter as they rode down Theobald Street. The sun flashing through the trees like a strobe light almost put her into a trance.

Her thoughts drifted back to the day before. She winced as the sight of Jimmy cradled by Jokerman on the blood-soaked sand kept flashing into her mind.

Pulling up outside Bishop's Supermarket, Terry turned to Judy.

"Are you sure that you can work today? You are bound to still be in shock. That's only natural. I can talk to the manager and explain, if you like. I can take you back to spend the day with my mum."

"That's thoughtful, love, but no thanks. I will be fine. Life must go on, and having witnessed those scenes yesterday, I am more determined than ever to make the most of life."

Judy had parcelled up her sad, grieving thoughts during the journey and put them to one side. Now, the gritty, ambitious Judy was taking over.

"OK, I'll pick you up at around 5.45pm, if that works for you," said Terry, smiling affectionately.

"That's fine, thanks. I think we should stop off on the way back and talk about the future—don't you?" replied Judy.

Terry nodded, blew her a kiss and set off to work.

The day passed slowly. Judy tried as hard as she could to put on a brave face, but despite her determination, she was still numb from the events of the last twenty-four hours. She felt that every customer that she served was staring at her as if they knew that she had been there in Margate when the Rocker was stabbed to death. It was all in her mind, of course, but she *had been* there, and the flashbacks continued. The event was on the front pages of all the newspapers. *Mods and Rockers Riot in Margate*, said one. *Rocker stabbed to death in Margate*, said another.

By the end of the day, she was physically and emotionally exhausted. Terry picked her up after work, and they stopped off at the Cat and Fiddle pub to talk things through, as they had agreed that morning.

They had a long discussion, tearing up beer mats nervously into ashtrays as they explored every option for the future. Suddenly, Terry jumped up and dropped to one knee. He held her hand and said softly,

"Marry me, Judy. We love each other—we don't need to wait. We can do it quickly, then find a flat somewhere. We are strong together; we can achieve anything we want to, as long as we are together."

This took Judy by complete surprise. She hadn't expected a proposal. She hadn't been tested, so she didn't know for certain that she was pregnant. She had not even intimated a concern on that front to Terry.

This was an unexpected but hugely welcome bonus. She loved Terry very much, and this unexpected proposal killed two birds with one stone. No need to go home again, and, if, as she believed, she was pregnant, they would start married life as a young family. The pub was full of drinkers on their way home after work stopping for a quick chat and a pint. The place fell silent immediately. Everyone turned, surveying the scene, waiting in anticipation for her response. She took a deep breath, then jumped up, nodding an acceptance.

She flung her arms around him and yelled, "Yes! Yes! Yes!"

They kissed passionately, oblivious to the audience looking on. Spontaneously, the drinkers in the pub cheered and applauded the happy couple. After all, it is not every night a proposal is made in a pub.

They raced home full of excitement and told Terry's parents that very evening. His parents expressed concern that they were rushing things but accepted that they made a great couple.

Terry and Judy were in no mood to heed any concerns. They just wanted to fix a date to get married as soon as possible. They didn't want any fuss, just a simple ceremony at Watford's registry office. They needed both sets of parents to sign their approval, as they were both under twenty-one years old—the age of consent. Judy privately threatened her parents with the exposure of her pregnancy almost two years ago, their banishment of her to Ireland and the forced adoption. They quickly agreed to give their approval, still fearful of the embarrassment the village would bestow upon them if the truth came out.

The wedding was arranged for Friday 11th June

Terry and Judy were determined and ambitious and wasted no time at all laying out their future together. Deciding to move far enough away to be independent but close enough to stay in touch with Terry's parents, they found a flat that they could afford to rent in Langley, Slough. Judy had made her mark at Bishop's, gaining a good reputation as a delicatessen manager, and she secured a transfer as a management trainee to the Bishop's Supermarket in Langley. It was a bigger store than the one in Radlett, with a very busy delicatessen department.

Terry was offered an interview with a top London corporate law firm. He impressed them so much that they hired him with a sponsorship to University College London (UCL) to take his law degree. He would start work immediately in London, commencing his course at UCL in September.

Terry's dad bought them a Mini Minor as a wedding present, which meant that he could keep his beloved scooter.

The couple's determination to carve out a future together impressed everyone. After a quiet wedding attended by both sets of parents, along with Nester, Jackie and the rest of the small Mod gang, they moved to Slough to start married life on Saturday, 12th June 1965. They spent their honeymoon night in a Watford hotel. Terry was over the moon and not at all concerned that Judy had agreed to marry him on the back of seeing Jimmy killed. He was delighted that he had the girl of his dreams. Judy loved Terry with all her heart.

Wednesday 16th June 1964

Jimmy's funeral had been arranged for 11am at Garston Crematorium. Word of the funeral had reached Terry, Judy and the Mod gang. They agreed that they should attend in a non-conspicuous way to show their respect for Jimmy.

In the two weeks that followed the stabbing at Margate, an autopsy revealed that the knife had pierced Jimmy's heart and that he had died instantly. The whole gory incident was described in bloody detail at the coroner's inquest, which concluded that Jimmy had been brutally murdered. The body was released for the funeral. The police had arrested a sixteen-year-old boy from Bermondsey, South London. After further investigation, he was charged with Jimmy's murder.

Jokerman, Turd, Terry and Nester met in the week before the funeral and agreed that the small Mod gang from Radlett, including Judy, would attend the funeral at a respectful distance.

Ironically, Jokerman and Nester had struck up a friendship on the back of the tragedy. It was a friendship that would last for the rest of their lives, despite their Mod and Rocker differences.

Terry and Judy picked up Nester and Jackie in Radlett in their small mini. The others made their way to the crematorium via car. It was important that there was not a scooter in sight. When they arrived at the crematorium gates, they were amazed at the number of motorcycles that had arrived.

It was a lovely clear, sunny day. There were over two hundred motorcycles lining the entrance to the crematorium.

Their petrol tanks gleamed in the sunlight, revealing all different makes of motorcycle. Royal Enfield, Norton, BSA, Vincent, Indian, AJS/Matchless, Velocette and, of course, Jimmy's favourite Triumphs. It was an amazing sight to behold. The funeral of a twenty-year-old man always attracted large numbers of mourners, but the funeral of a young biker attracted bikers from the clubs all over London. Bikers from the 59 Club, The Ace Café, The Busy Bee and even the Ryka's lot from Box Hill turned up to mourn Jimmy's passing.

The hearse, followed by just one car carrying Jimmy's distraught mother, pulled in through the crematorium gates. The funeral director stepped out of the hearse. He stood in front of it, bowed his head and began to lead the procession down the long driveway to the main hall.

It was an extraordinary sight—over two hundred bikers were dressed in their leather jackets, white silk scarves, white T-shirts, blue denim jeans and knee-high biker boots topped with white socks. They stood next to their bikes en route down the driveway, each bowing their heads as the hearse carrying Jimmy's coffin passed.

Jokerman had travelled in the car with Jimmy's mother as her main support. She had asked him to dress in his biker's gear.

She faltered and almost stumbled as he helped her into the crematorium. They were followed by as many bikers as could fit into the main hall. Turd had arranged for Terry, Judy and the rest of the group to go in last, upstairs in the gallery.

The service began with Elvis Presley singing 'Long Black Limousine'. The tears began to flow as Elvis's voice rang out through the loudspeakers.

Big, burly bikers were wiping tears from their eyes as they remembered a fellow biker. Jokerman delivered a eulogy to his best friend, describing him as a free spirit who loved rock and roll and the open road. Then he paused, looked up at the gallery and caught Judy's eye. She was shaking her head slowly, visibly trembling, willing him in her mind not to mention her. After a pause he moved on.

He spent some time highlighting the relationship Jimmy had enjoyed in his short life with his mother. He praised Jimmy's mother for raising such a great lad without a husband, who had tragically been killed before Jimmy was born at the end of the Second World War. Finally, he finished with Jimmy's zest for all things to do with motorbikes—especially Triumph motorbikes.

His voice wavered, and he fought back the tears when he said, "Farewell, my best friend."

The service finished with Frank Ifield singing 'The Wayward Wind'. Terry, Judy and the gang slipped out the front, avoiding the biker congregation out the back looking over the wreaths from many biker clubs. The biggest one was from all the boys and girls at The Busy Bee, with a card that read, 'Rest in peace, Jimmy, the leader of the pack.'

Monday 21st June 1965

Terry got home from work late that evening. It was seven pm. Judy had rustled up a spaghetti bolognese. They sat down to eat, still pinching themselves that they were married. Getting on with their lives away from their parents was a challenge that they relished.

Judy had missed her period and had suppressed any morning sickness for almost a month.

They were chatting away when she said, "Terry, I don't know how best to put this, but I haven't had my period since our holiday. I think I may be pregnant."

Terry's face was a picture; his eyes and his mouth were wide open, and a piece of spaghetti hung from his lip. He didn't know how to react to this news. Was he supposed to be shocked, happy, worried, scared, or just plain flabbergasted? Inside, he was bursting with joy and excitement despite the challenges that they would face.

"Crikey," he yelled with an expression of delight on his face, "that's fantastic! I don't care how hard it will be—we can face it together. It's much sooner than I expected to have a family, but who cares? We can do it together."

Judy looked at Terry and smiled. She loved his can-do attitude.

"I thought you might be shocked, or even angry," she said with a grin.

"Bloody hell, no! I'm excited and a little scared for the responsibility. When can you get tested? When will we know for sure?"

"I'll book an appointment with our new doctor and get a test. Hopefully we will find out sometime at the end of next week. In the meantime, we can plan things ourselves, but we must not tell anyone until we know one way or another for certain. Agreed?"

"Agreed," replied Terry with a smug look on his face.

Wednesday 30th June 1965

Judy finished work at 1.30pm. It was a half-day closing at Bishop's supermarket in Langley. She had an appointment with the local doctor to find out the results of her pregnancy test. She knew her own body; in her mind, this test was just to confirm what she already knew.

Sure enough, the doctor confirmed that Judy was pregnant, and from what she had told him, he concluded that her baby would be due in late February 1966. She skipped out of the surgery and went back to the flat to wait for Terry to get home to tell him the news.

Terry was as pleased as Judy at the news, and they set about planning for the future. She would go back to work after the baby was born.

Two incomes, after baby minder fees, would help put Terry through university even though he had sponsorship. Judy was convinced that she could carve out a career at Bishop's in fresh food. She was good at it—she had an instinct and a passion for retailing.

She also didn't think that the competition from her peer group was that strong. She had ambitions to get into marketing and buying at head office. Her pregnancy and childrearing would have to fit around those plans.

In the months that followed, they worked hard. Their mod days seemed a distant past, apart from the odd dinner party with Nester and Jackie. They got evening work at the local pub to subsidise their income.

By Christmas 1965, Judy was seven months pregnant. They spent Christmas Day with Terry's parents, who were delighted at the prospect of their first grandchild.

Judy had hardly seen her parents since the wedding. Her feelings towards them had not improved with time. She had, however, let them know that she was expecting a child in February.

'California Dreamin'' by The Mamas and The Papas was number one in the charts in January 1966. The Mod scene was developing fast, and female fashions became much more revealing. The miniskirt, an invention credited to designer Mary Quant, was dominating the scene. The advent of tights rendered the suspender belt redundant. All the boys thought that tights were passion killers, although practical for women. 1966 was also the year that a young, thin model nicknamed Twiggy hit the scene. She quickly became the face of female Mods.

Although Judy still had a keen interest in clothes and fashion, she was now getting very large. It would not be long before she and Terry would have a little life to care for.

Saturday 26th February 1966

Judy had left work two weeks earlier. She knew that her baby would be born any day. They woke up. It was 7am.

Terry went to make a cup of tea when he heard Judy shout from the toilet, "Bloody hell, Terry, my waters have broken! The baby is coming!"

Terry dropped the teapot in panic, then ran to help Judy to the bedroom to get changed.

He bundled her into the mini and drove like a maniac to the hospital.

Judy was in the delivery room. It was not customary, in those days, for the father to be allowed into the delivery room to watch the birth. Terry sat outside, anxiously awaiting news.

Inside the delivery room, Judy was making good progress. The midwife was calling out instructions.

"That's right! Short breaths. Now give a big push—come on, push as hard as you can."

Judy was grunting and groaning. The top of the baby's head was visible.

"Next time, Judy, give one big push with the contraction, and your baby's head will appear. Come on, push hard!"

Judy did as she was told, and with her last push, a beautiful baby girl was born.

The midwife did all the necessary things with the umbilical cord. The baby let out a rasping cry.

Wrapped in a towel, a beautiful little girl was presented to Judy. She was weeping with joy. The first moment she saw her baby's face with her eyes open, Judy sobbed and sobbed. Partly joy, but mostly with the realisation that she had been denied this moment just over two years ago, when her baby was taken from her straight away. She put that to the back of her mind. Her life was with Terry now—and this beautiful little girl.

Terry was invited in to see his wife and his new daughter. They cried happy tears together.

At that moment, Judy and Terry realised that their responsibilities had changed. Their new, small family was now their priority.

It was the end of an era for them. Judy had been both a Rocker and a Mod. She and Terry had grown a relationship through a period of dramatic cultural change. The 60s were, indeed, a unique period of change after the war. They had enjoyed the experience but realised that they must move on with their lives and provide a great upbringing for their child.

In the 1960s, it was a common expectation that women would leave work upon falling pregnant. There were no maternity leave laws in place at that time. However, Judy was highly thought of by the directors at Bishop's Food Stores. They agreed to have her back after three months of unpaid leave. They gave her a role as a buying assistant at the Head Office in South Ruislip, which meant that she could have weekends at home.

Her career had begun. They named their baby Charlotte and set about building two careers and raising a baby together. It was tough. Judy attended night school at Slough College to do an HND (Higher National Diploma) in business studies. Terry got his law degree and went on to become a successful corporate lawyer at his firm, Linklaters, in the City of London.

By the time Charlotte was five years old, their careers had really taken off. However, they had been trying for another child for two years without success. This was very troubling; Judy was concerned that if, for some reason, Terry could not have children, then that would cause a great deal of trouble. What would she do if that were the case? The thought of it sent shivers down her spine. Terry was a wonderful man who she loved dearly, and she perished the thought of hurting him in any way.

They were about to go to the doctor and ask for help when Judy suddenly announced to Terry, "Honey my period is over three weeks late. I have booked a test with the doctor—fingers crossed!"

She was smiling with relief. Terry was delighted.

Sure enough, she was pregnant. Nine months later, she gave birth to a baby boy. They both agreed that he should be called James.

In 1977, they moved to Potters Bar in Hertfordshire so that Charlotte could go to secondary school in the area. James was now six and had finished his last year at infants' school in Potters Bar.

Judy had climbed the corporate ladder at Bishop's and became their Fresh Food Director in 1978. Terry had also been appointed the youngest partner at Linklaters law firm. Their income had improved so much that in 1980, they moved to a big house in Hadley Wood and sent both children to private schools.

In 1981, Judy's dad was found dead in his workshop. He died from a heart attack. He and Judy had never made up their differences.

Judy attended the funeral alone with her mum, who had now developed Alzheimer's disease. She went into a home in Shenley in 1982 and died two years later.

In 1984, Judy joined Tesco as a category director for fresh food and went on to complete twenty-one years' service, retiring in 2005.

Charlotte graduated from Oxford with a first in Classics. She went into politics and became a special advisor to the Blair government in 1997. She married a Labour MP in 2004. They lived in Hitchin, Hertfordshire. In 2005 Terry and Judy's first grandchild was born—a boy named Harry—and in 2007, their second grandchild was born. She was a little girl known as Patsy.

James graduated from Cambridge with a first in biochemistry. He went on to work for AstraZeneca, married a fellow scientist and had two children named Sarah and Jane, born in 2009 and 2011. They lived in Putney in London.

Tragedy struck the family in 2007. It was a devastating blow for Terry and Judy and changed their lives forever. Charlotte, her husband, her son Harry, aged two, and Patsy, aged six months, were travelling on the M6 to the Lake District. Their car was involved in a multiple pile-up and everyone in the car except Patsy, the baby, was killed instantly. Miraculously, Patsy escaped without injury, wrapped in her travel cot.

The papers carried the headline: MP and his family involved in multiple pile-up on the M6.

In all, fifteen people died in the accident, leaving the nation stunned.

Terry and Judy took Patsy under their wing and set about raising another child whilst grieving their enormous loss. Patsy grew up in Hadley Wood and went to the same private school that her mother had years before. Terry was known to Patsy as Papa Terry, and Judy was Grandma. She could not remember her immediate family, as she was so young when they were killed.

Patsy loved spending her early years listening to Papa Terry telling her stories of when he and her grandma were young, growing up in Borehamwood and Letchmore Heath. She particularly liked helping Papa Terry clean his Lambretta GT 200, which he still had in his garage in Hadley Wood. Terry had restored the scooter with modern brakes. It was in pristine condition and was his pride and joy.

Terry retired in 2008 at the age of 60 on a handsome pension from a life spent at his law firm. In his retirement, he spent a great deal of time helping to raise Patsy, who had come to live with them at just six months of age. Patsy loved her Papa Terry because he was always teasing her and joking around, whereas Grandma was the strict one, making sure that she did as she was told, studied hard and had ambitions for the future.

It was a massive blow to Patsy when, at the age of ten, her Papa Terry was killed in a road accident riding his scooter with his old mates. Nester and Little Pete were out with Terry for one of their memory lane rides when Terry was hit by an overtaking lorry. He didn't stand a chance. The lorry narrowly missed taking out Nester and Little Pete in the process.

The lorry driver was sentenced to six years in prison for causing death by dangerous driving.

This was some small comfort to Judy and Patsy, who were distraught at the loss of a great guy. Judy struggled heavily with her grief, although she knew that she could not dwell on her sadness, as Patsy was her complete priority now.

At Terry's funeral, Nester gave a eulogy straight after one given by one of Terry's ex-partners at Linklaters.

The contrast was stark. First, Terry was described as the consummate corporate lawyer who had led teams through many large corporate transactions in the City of London. He was described as someone who had run marathons all his life, raising millions of pounds for charity. A consummate professional at all times.

When Nester stood up, he described the kid he grew up with. As he recalled their bird's nesting escapades and their camaraderie as Mods in the early sixties, some laughter was generated—especially when he described how he and Terry had got their own back on the Rockers at The Busy Bee by chaining their bikes together. The lawyer folk looked at one another in surprise, whilst Jokerman nodded and gave a wry smile from the back. Terry was cremated at the age of sixty-nine.

The Reveal

Judy went on to raise Patsy on her own. Although she loved all her grandchildren, Patsy held a special place in her heart because she had never known her parents. Judy worked hard to ensure that Patsy was exposed to as many opportunities as possible. Horse riding, ballet, swimming, gymnastics and other extracurricular activities such as the theatre became the order of the day. Judy was her coach, mentor, substitute mother and a wise old grandma to boot. It was a busy period throughout Patsy's early teenage years. The bond between the two of them was immense.

One day, just before the Covid pandemic broke out, Judy was contacted by someone associated with the Magdalene Laundries in Ireland. Judy kept this approach a secret from Patsy because she had never told the story of her first child to anyone.

"Is that Judy McDermott?" asked the voice on the other end of the phone.

"Yes, but I am Judy King now," came the reply.

"Oh, good. My name is Jennifer Kitchen. I represent the lawyers looking at the Magdalene Laundry scandals as far back as the 1950s. Have you got a moment to talk?"

"Of course," responded Judy nervously, thankful that Patsy was at school.

Judy's heart was beating frantically, as she had no clue what the stranger was going to say.

"Well, Judy—may I call you Judy?"

"Of course," said Judy in an urgent voice.

"Well, Judy. We have been contacted by a woman who was adopted from the Magdalene Laundry in Dublin in 1963. We believe, from the records that were kept at the time, that she is, in fact, your daughter."

The silence was deafening. Judy was shaking like a leaf; her hand that held the phone was trembling so much that she put the call on speaker and rested the handset on the coffee table. She could see her reflection in the mirror on the wall. The colour had drained completely from her face. She looked like she had seen a ghost.

Digging deep, Judy summoned up some courage from somewhere within her and responded, "Are you sure?"

"Yes, Judy, we are sure. Everything checks out. This lady is your daughter. Her name is Elizabeth Hill. That is her married name— she was formally Elizabeth Byers. She is now fifty-six years old."

"Crikey, I don't know what to say. I'm in shock. Please, can I let this sink in for a bit?"

Judy wanted to be happy, but knowing about the daughter that was taken from her so brutally all those years ago was also going to be very painful.
"No problem, Judy. Take your time."

After a few minutes, Judy cleared her throat.

"Thank you for the call. What is it that Elizabeth wants you to say to me?"

She knew the answer but did not want to be presumptuous.

"Elizabeth, or Lizzy, as she is known, wants to be put in touch and eventually meet with her maternal mother. By the way, we have permission from her to tell you her name, although she does not know your name yet. The purpose of my call is to introduce you to this request. Once you have had time to reflect and have made your decision as to whether you want to facilitate her request, we can move to stage two," Jennifer said. She was softly spoken with a caring voice.

"Stage two. And what might that be?" Judy mused. She looked to the ceiling and tutted at the stupidity of her question; of course she could work out for herself what stage two would be.

"Stage two, Judy, would be for us to provide you with information about Lizzy—background, family, career, hobbies—that sort of thing. We would provide similar information about you to Lizzy."

Jennifer sounded quite formal now.

"OK, and stage three?" asked Judy, again looking skyward at the simplicity of her question.

"Stage three, Judy, would be for you to meet each other."

Judy was calmer now. Her heart had returned to a normal beat, but her hands were sticky with sweat.

"Can you give me a few days to let this all sink in, please? We can chat again. I don't want to rush into making decisions today, if that is alright."

"Of course, Judy. I'll call you in two days' time. What time of day is best for you?"

"Around 2pm is best for me. Thank you for calling, and I look forward to speaking again."

"OK. Thanks, Judy. Goodbye."

Judy sat, almost paralysed by the news. Of course, her instinct was to agree to everything. She wanted to meet and hug the daughter that she had thought about every day of her life since 1963. Not a day had gone by since the birth that Judy had not wondered what had become of the little baby girl whose face she had never seen. Her thoughts went back to the brutality of the nuns in taking her baby so quickly. But—and there is always a 'but'—what would be the ramifications of getting to know each other after all this time? Would Lizzy resent Judy for giving her up without a fight? Would it be too painful for them both? How would she tell the rest of the family, and how would they react? Questions! So many questions.

Judy spent some time thinking it through and decided long before the next call that she would agree to moving to the next stage.

And so started a process that one day might result in her meeting her lost daughter.

Judy supplied all the relevant information about herself to Jennifer Kitchen and then waited to receive similar information about Lizzy.

Patsy was at school when the recorded delivery envelope arrived from Jennifer Kitchen.

She looked at the envelope for a moment, not sure if she was ready to find out all about her long-lost daughter.

Suddenly, she was reliving all the hurt, the despair that she went through. She thought about how wretched she felt at the time. Her resentment towards her parents resurfaced in her mind.

How could they have put their only daughter through such an ordeal? Then she thought of Terry. How she longed for him to be with her at that moment. He would have been a pillar of strength in her hour of need. She smiled at the thought, knowing that his memory would give her the strength required to open the envelope.

After a couple of minutes, she took a deep breath and ripped open the package.

'Details of Elizabeth, known as Lizzy Hill, formally Elizabeth Byers.'

There was a picture of her which captured Judy's gaze for ten minutes or more. Tears rolled down her face. She smiled—here, in front of her, was her lost daughter Charlotte peering through the face of this woman. This troubled her, as it meant that Charlotte had almost certainly been Jimmy's daughter and not

Terry's. Despite never running any tests to find out the truth, she had often thought to herself that Charlotte was Jimmy's child. What was the point back then, she thought; Jimmy was dead, and she loved Terry so much. Everything had turned out for the best. Terry was a wonderful father to Charlotte.

Then she read the notes:

'Adopted from Magdalene Laundry by Mr and Mrs Byers, 27 Grove Street, Cheltenham, Gloucestershire.

Born Wednesday, 10th June 1964.

Place of birth: Magdalene Laundry, Killarney Street, Dublin. Only child adopted by Sam and Grace Byers.

Secondary School: Balcarras School, Charlton Kings, Cheltenham.

University Magdalen College Oxford: first-class degree in English.

Married to Clive Hill, a barrister and Queen's Counsel.

Two Children: Stephen Hill, born 2003, and Susan Hill, born 2005.

Career: teacher of English.

Hobbies: all kinds of sport, reading and the theatre.'

It was a short description, but enough for Judy to realise that she had had a good upbringing and had enjoyed a relatively successful life so far.

Judy gazed at her picture and wondered if meeting up was a good thing. She had lots of questions for Jennifer Kitchen for next time they spoke.

Out of the blue, the Covid pandemic struck, slowing everything to a grinding halt. Lockdown didn't help, as it rendered any kind of meeting impossible. After exchanging mobile phone details via Jennifer Kitchen, both Judy and Lizzy decided to chat over the phone using WhatsApp video.

Tuesday 2nd March 2021

The call came in. It was 2pm, and Patsy was at school. Judy braced herself to see her long-lost daughter for the first time in her life. There she was on the screen. Judy could see Jimmy in her straight away. She gasped.

Much to her embarrassment, she immediately burst into tears, shaking her head and saying, "I'm sorry. I'm so, so sorry for letting you go, but I had no choice. Please understand!"

Lizzy smiled, and it was as if Jimmy was smiling at her.

"Don't worry, Judy. You don't have to feel sorry. I've read all about those awful Magdalene Laundries; it must have been so difficult for someone so young. I had a loving and wonderful upbringing. There is nothing for you to feel sorry about."

Judy gathered her composure and noticed that Lizzy's eyes were also welling up with tears.

"Thank you, Lizzy. It sounds like your adopted parents did a great job. Are they still around?"

"Sadly not, I'm afraid. They were in their late thirties when they adopted me. They both died in their nineties, but they had long and fulfilled lives."

"I'm sorry to hear that. Where do you live these days? Are we allowed to ask that? I'm not sure what stage we are at regarding this reunion. There seems to be a protocol to follow, but my emotions are running away with me at the moment."

"I don't think stages or protocol matter now, Judy. I'm so happy to meet you, even by video, and would like to get to know you better once this pandemic is out of the way.

I see that you have three grandchildren. I was very sorry to hear about the dreadful loss of your daughter and most of her family."

"Yes, that was a dreadful experience. It was over 14 years ago now. None of us should ever have to attend our own child's funeral, let alone that of almost a whole family," sighed Judy.

"Well, I suppose you technically have two more grandchildren now. But all in good time. Who knows? You might get to meet them one day."

"Yes, all in good time. I'd like that."

Judy was already feeling that things were going well, but she did not want them to go too fast.

They ended the call and agreed to do more WhatsApp calls until they found a time when they could meet up.

Later that year, Judy felt unwell and had bowel problems. After a visit to the doctor, she was signed up for a colonoscopy to investigate what might be causing her symptoms. Judy told Patsy that she was going for tests on her gut, as she put it. Patsy was alarmed. Apart from Uncle James and her cousins, she had nobody else, and she was frightened for her grandma. Patsy's concern was well-founded, as the results of the colonoscopy identified a problem. Judy was immediately admitted to hospital for a colectomy operation to remove cancer from her colon.

She was put on a course of chemotherapy. The surgeon told Judy that, although they had removed the cancer from her colon, it had spread to her bones, and, unfortunately, she may only have two or three years to live depending on the success of subsequent treatments.

Judy decided not to tell her son, James, or Patsy what the surgeon had said.

During the next three years, Judy's condition deteriorated, despite continuous treatments. She braced herself to tell James and Patsy how ill she was. She also told Lizzy of her condition and diagnosis. They had not had time to meet since the pandemic due to Judy's illness and because Lizzy lived in St Albans, so they decided now to make an effort to meet up.

Stark Reality

Tuesday 16th April 2024

They met for lunch at Sopwell House Hotel in St Albans. It was a successful lunch, and they talked about everything. The past, Lizzy's biological father Jimmy Tucker, Judy's late husband and all the family. After lunch, they visited the washroom. Lizzy brushed her hair and popped into the loo, leaving her brush by the washbasin. Judy quickly gathered some of Lizzy's hair from the brush, wrapped it in tissue paper and popped it into her bag.

Over coffee, they talked about Judy's health. They decided that the potential turmoil from introducing their respective families to the truth might be too much for Judy as she battled with her illness. They decided to leave it a secret between them for now.

When Judy went home, she recovered a lock of Charlotte's hair that she had kept after she was killed. She decided to get a DNA test done to establish if they were both Jimmy's children. When the results came through, she decided that she must share her story with James and Patsy. But first, she needed to talk to Lizzy.

During the next four months, Judy's condition deteriorated fast. She had not had a chance to speak to anyone about her past or recent findings. She was admitted to the Watford Peace Hospice, and, inevitably, her health deteriorated further. James was encouraged to take a pre-planned two-month holiday in America with his family. Judy hoped that she could hang on until his return and introduce everyone to her past. But, as time slipped by, that looked like it was not going to be possible.

Autumn 2024

Patsy finished college early. She got to the hospice at 4pm, as her grandma had requested. She was intrigued to see her grandma and find out what things she wanted her to know. As she walked through the door of the hospice, the receptionist asked her to wait, as one of the doctors wanted to see her. 'That's not good,' she thought. She didn't have to wait long before being ushered into a room with a nurse and a doctor.

"Patsy, your grandmother has deteriorated today. She is very weak. There is every chance that she might slip away this evening or overnight," the doctor explained.

Patsy had been expecting this type of news for the last two weeks. She knew that her grandma was a fighter and that she would cling on to life as long as she could, but she feared the worst when she had left that morning.

"Thank you, doctor, for letting me know. I will be careful not to trouble her too much. But this morning she asked me to return early this evening because she has things to tell me. If that is important for her, I will just hold her hand and listen."

"OK, Patsy. You know where we are if you need us," the nurse said sympathetically.

Patsy made her way to her grandma's room. She was shocked at how gaunt she had started to look since that morning. As she sat down beside the bed, she gently held her grandma's hand. Judy opened her eyes and smiled.

"Hello, love. You made it early, I see. Thanks for that. Have you had a good day?"

"Yes, Grandma, but it's important that you rest."

"Ah, rubbish. You've been talking to the doctor. I've got things to share with you—important things that you need to know, love. You need to promise me that you will tell these things to your Uncle James when he gets back from holiday, OK?

"Yes, Grandma. I promise."

Patsy was very concerned; her grandma had never spoken as if she wasn't going to be here before.

Judy started her story, beginning with her first meeting with Jimmy Tucker, the handsome Rocker at the local shop on the first day she started her hairdressing course at Casio College. Patsy listened intently; she had never heard her grandma talk so intimately about anyone other than Papa Terry before.

Judy went on, covering her fallout with her parents, discovering that she was pregnant, being dumped in Ireland with her Auntie Erin and eventually finding herself discarded in the Magdalene Laundry.

Patsy was shocked, but not surprised, as she always knew that her grandma was a bit of a free spirit as a teenager.

However, she had no idea that she had been pregnant or that the child was taken away from her to be adopted before she even saw the baby's face.

Tears began to roll down Patsy's face, as she could see that telling her story was a relief for Judy after years of keeping secrets. Judy continued with her story, recalling how she met Terry when she returned to England and how his real name had been Jess. Patsy interrupted her tears with laughter when Judy told her why the name Terry stuck.

"Cocky sod, he was pretending it was fate that we met. He had a J on his scooter, and, of course, my name began with a J. I had to smile. It was a great chat-up line, but when he conned me by saying his name was Terry, I made him live with it. All his friends accepted my demands. That's how your Papa Terry went from Jess to Terry; it truly stuck for the rest of his life."

She went on to describe how long it had taken for her to get passionate with Terry, even though she grew to love him so much. When she outlined how she had had non-consensual sex with Jimmy on the day she finally finished with him for good, Patsy was shocked and very angry at the Jimmy that was being described.

The storytelling continued with the holiday camp freedom and her first real time having sex with papa Terry , which was also unprotected. Patsy laughed at the description of the scenes at the holiday camp, especially imagining Judy on top of the rostrum as Miss Maddison in the beauty contest.

Patsy let out a yelp when Judy described the scenes at Margate and the death of Jimmy the biker.

She shook her head in amazement at the teenage life her grandma had led.

"When your mum was born, I sensed that she was possibly Jimmy's daughter, but I couldn't be sure. Your Papa Terry was hellbent on marrying me, anyway. Charlotte could well have been his daughter, so we set up home together. Papa Terry was a wonderful father to your mum; they loved each other very much indeed."

Patsy was on the edge of her seat now, her head reeling. What else could her grandma possibly tell her?

Judy went on to tell Patsy how Lizzy, her firstborn daughter, had gotten in touch a few years ago. She described how the pandemic had slowed down contact between them, but how, eventually, they had met.

Judy was getting weaker now, struggling to talk and occasionally gasping for breath. She beckoned Patsy to come closer.

"You see, Patsy I managed to get some hair from Lizzy's hairbrush when we were in the washroom. I had a lock of your mum's hair at home, so I was able to do a DNA test. The result came through. Your mum and Lizzy were sisters. Jimmy the biker was their father. So, you see, you have more family out there than just Uncle James and his family."

Patsy was speechless. She had spent the whole day wondering what her grandma wanted to tell her. She concluded that a person could not make this stuff up; it was extraordinary.

Judy was down to a soft whisper at this point. She tried to pull Patsy closer to hear what she had to say next.

"You see, Patsy, dear, I've left details in my filing cabinet at home. Your aunty Lizzy lives in St Albans. She is married to Clive Hill, and they have two children. Stephen is 21 and Susan is 19. Get in touch when I'm gone. Tell Uncle James this story for me, love, please."

Judy was struggling for air. Suddenly, she stopped breathing and drifted away. Patsy was numb with shock—and not just because her dear grandmother had just passed. She jumped up and got the nurses. She was crying now. After a moment spent staring at her beloved grandma's face, tears blurring her vision, Patsy ran down the corridor to the front door.

Lizzy is short for Elizabeth. Clive and Elizabeth Hill in St Albans—that's Brad's parents' name. Brad is his second name; he prefers it to his first name, Stephen. He has a sister called Susan. Brad. Brad, the boy she had been seeing. The boy she had only, just now, texted...

She was running to the door, sobbing hard. As she got to the door she ran outside and looked to the car park. There was Brad coming towards her. She realised that this very special guy was in fact her first cousin! She threw back her head, outstretched her hands, arched her back and yelled at the top of her voice into the night sky...

"Help!"